If Dr. Kat Macauley thought he'd go away just because she threw up a few roadblocks, she'd seriously underestimated him

Seth was determined to get to the bottom of this counterfeiting case. And if Kat was behind it, she'd end up in prison, where she belonged.

But what about the kid?

If the kid was his, he'd do the right thing. He'd make sure she was taken care of. He'd been a foster child, shunted from family to family until he'd escaped at eighteen, and no child of his would suffer that way.

Trouble was, he didn't have a clue about raising kids. Whether Macauley was guilty or not, what the hell was he going to do if the girl really *was* his?

Dear Reader,

How would a man react if he found out he had a daughter he hadn't known existed? He'd probably be angry that he hadn't been told, but how would he decide what was best for his child? What if he was asked to sign papers terminating his parental rights and to walk away, leaving her in a loving home? What would he do?

What about the woman who wants to adopt the child? How would she feel when the girl's biological father showed up? She'd be terrified that she was going to lose the child she loved–and that her little girl, still grieving for her mother, was going to be handed over to a stranger.

The love we feel for our children is fierce and all-consuming. We would do anything for them, give anything we had to protect them from pain and suffering. In *Stranger in a Small Town,* Kat and Seth have to struggle to find a way to become a family–but nothing so important is ever easy.

This is the last book in my Small Town series. I hate to say goodbye to Sturgeon Falls and all the people who live there, but I had a wonderful time writing Kat and Seth and Regan's story. No matter how a family is formed, the bonds that tie them together are unbreakable. And the love we draw from our families is the most powerful force on earth.

Margaret Watson

P.S. I love to hear from my readers! Visit me at my Web site, www.margaretwatson.com, or e-mail me at mwatson1004@hotmail.com.

STRANGER IN A
SMALL TOWN
Margaret Watson

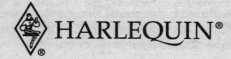

HARLEQUIN®

TORONTO • NEW YORK • LONDON
AMSTERDAM • PARIS • SYDNEY • HAMBURG
STOCKHOLM • ATHENS • TOKYO • MILAN • MADRID
PRAGUE • WARSAW • BUDAPEST • AUCKLAND

ISBN-13: 978-0-373-71461-2
ISBN-10: 0-373-71461-0

STRANGER IN A SMALL TOWN

www.eHarlequin.com

Printed in U.S.A.

ABOUT THE AUTHOR

Margaret Watson has always made up stories in her head. When she started actually writing them down, she realized that she'd found exactly what she wanted to do with the rest of her life. Fifteen years after staring at that first blank page, she's written nineteen books for Silhouette and Harlequin Books and has been twice nominated for the prestigious RITA® Award.

When she's not writing or spending time with her family, she practices veterinary medicine. Besides the tremendous satisfaction in her job, it provides the inspiration for wonderful characters and interesting stories. Margaret lives in a Chicago suburb with her husband and three daughters and a menagerie of pets.

Books by Margaret Watson

HARLEQUIN SUPERROMANCE

Don't miss any of our special offers. Write to us at the following address for information on our newest releases.

Harlequin Reader Service
U.S.: 3010 Walden Ave., P.O. Box 1325, Buffalo, NY 14269
Canadian: P.O. Box 609, Fort Erie, Ont. L2A 5X3

For my family—my husband, Bill,
and my daughters, Katy, Chelsea and Meg.
You are everything to me.

PROLOGUE

THE WOMAN ON THE BED STIRRED and her eyes fluttered open. "Kat."

The hoarse whisper was barely more than a breath in the dim, silent room, and Katriona Macauley gently took her friend's hand. "I'm here, Holly."

"Have they found him?"

"Not yet."

"I'm scared, Kat."

Kat smoothed a finger over Holly's cheek. Her skin was as dry and thin as paper, a fragile covering for even more fragile bones. "I know," she murmured. "I'm scared, too."

"Regan won't understand. She'll be so frightened." Holly struggled to swallow. "She'll need you, Kat. Promise me you'll take care of her."

"You know I will, sweetie," Kat crooned, her voice thickening. "I promise." She leaned closer so that Holly could see her eyes. "I'll make sure she knows how much you loved her. And she'll know that I love her, too."

"What if Seth won't sign the papers?" Holly moved restlessly.

"Why wouldn't he? He told you he didn't want children. When the agency finds him, he'll sign the papers."

"He'll be angry."

"The adoption agency knows you looked for him. They'll tell him. He'll understand."

"I hope so." Holly shifted, each movement bringing a pained look to her worn face. "I need the pictures."

"Which pictures?" Kat asked.

"In the drawer."

"In the desk?"

"Underwear drawer." Holly's mouth lifted in a ghost of her old mischievous grin. "Where we always hid the important stuff."

Her eyes closed and Kat's answering smile vanished. Holly had already begun to disappear. Her skin looked yellow and lifeless against the green sheet, and Kat felt a familiar flash of anger. Why Holly? Why had the disease chosen the laughing, vibrant young woman as its victim? Why was Regan going to be left an orphan?

But Kat's anger wouldn't help Holly. Or Regan. Swallowing the hard knot of fear and grief, Kat opened the top drawer of Holly's dresser. Her throat closed as she reached beneath the colorful scraps of silk that Holly wouldn't wear again.

The manila envelope was pushed all the way to the back. As she drew it out, Kat saw *Regan* scrawled on the front in Holly's distinctive handwriting.

"Holly? I found the envelope."

"Open it," Holly said, her eyes still closed.

Kat flattened the metal clasp and opened the envelope. Regan's birth certificate slid out, along with a handful of photos.

"Is this Seth Anderson?" The pictures were of Holly and a man. An attractive man with dark brown hair and brown eyes who had draped his arm over Holly's shoulder. Smiling, he held a beer up as if toasting the camera. Kat studied the picture, trying to ignore the tiny zing of interest. "Regan's father?"

"Yes. Those are the only photos I have. Keep them safe for Regan."

"I will." Kat heard the screech of the school bus's brakes grinding outside and gently blotted the tears off Holly's face. "There's the bus. Regan's home. You don't want her to see you crying."

"Don't let her see me like this, Kat," Holly whispered. "I don't want her to remember me this way."

"She doesn't care what you look like," Kat

answered. "You're her mother, and she loves you."
Kat held the glass with the straw to Holly's mouth so
she could take a drink. "Regan needs to be with you."

One last tear rolled down Holly's face. "I need her,
too," Holly whispered. "I want my baby."

TWO WEEKS LATER, KAT STOOD next to an open grave,
gripping Regan's hand tightly. The girl stared at the
burnished wooden casket, her eyes unreadable.

A sharp April wind sliced through the trees, dis-
lodging raindrops from the previous night's storm.
One landed on Regan's cheek and slid down, mim-
icking a tear, and Kat brushed it away.

Regan hadn't shed any tears since her mother had
died.

The minister completed the service, and the
mourners drifted over to Kat and Regan, murmuring
words of sympathy. Some of them bent to speak to
Regan, but she looked at them with her dark blue
eyes and didn't answer.

Finally, only Kat's parents and her friend Charlotte Burns were left. Her father, Gus, wrapped one
arm around her shoulders. "Let's get you and Regan
home," he said, his voice gruff. "It looks as if it's
going to storm again."

As they drove away from the cemetery, Regan
said, "Kat?" The child's voice sounded almost rusty

with disuse. She'd spoken very little since her mother had died.

"Yes, honey?"

"Is Mommy going to be cold? It's cold outside, and she wasn't wearing a coat."

Oh, dear God. What could she say? How could she expect a child to understand the bitter finality of death? "Your mommy is with God now, Regan. God won't let her get cold."

"She's not with God. I saw her. I saw her in that box." Regan's face tightened as if she were going to cry.

"The part of her that's still alive, the part that's really your mom, is with God. Her body is just the part that's left behind." Kat tucked a strand of dark blond hair behind Regan's ear. "Don't you remember that from Sunday school?"

Regan scowled. "That's stupid."

Kat didn't want to accept that Holly had died. Why should a six-year-old girl? She pulled Regan as close as her seat belt would allow. "We'll never stop loving your mom. She won't live with us anymore, but we'll always remember her. We'll look at the pictures we put in the photo albums and the letters she wrote you. All we have to do is think about her, and she'll be with us."

Regan's mouth quivered. "I don't want her to go. I want her to be with us."

"I know, honey," Kat said softly. "So do I."

Regan studied Kat with wary eyes. "Are you going to leave, too?"

"Never." Kat held the little girl more tightly. "I'm never going to leave you, Regan. I promise."

CHAPTER ONE

October, Washington D.C.

"DAMN IT!"

The muscles in Seth Anderson's leg spasmed. Trying to ease the pain, he straightened his knee, but the movement only made it worse.

"Seth? You okay?" The man in the next cubicle peered around the corner.

"Fine," Seth said between his teeth. "Thanks."

"Yell if you need anything." The other agent scooted his chair back into his own space.

Yell. Seth closed his eyes. He was doing his damnedest *not* to yell.

The cramp finally released and Seth slumped back, waiting for the waves of pain to recede. When he was sure he could stand, he grabbed the cane next to his desk and lurched to his feet. With grim satisfaction, he walked down the corridor to the water fountain.

He might be slow, he might be unsteady, but he was walking.

The doctors had told him he'd never walk again.

By the time he returned to his desk, sweat ran down his back and his leg was trembling. But he'd managed to get his own glass of water without having to ask anyone to get it for him. Progress.

"Hey, Seth." Brian Carlson, the section supervisor, appeared in his cubicle. "How's it going?"

"Good. I'm good."

Brian dropped into the chair next to Seth's desk and nodded at the folders spread out in front of him. "Find anything for me?"

Seth had braced for a question about his leg. Relieved, he shook his head. "Not a thing. So far it looks as if your agents have covered all the bases."

"I know you don't want to be here," Brian said, drumming his fingers on the desk. "That you want to get back to the protection detail." Brian didn't repeat what the doctors had told him, that Seth would never be healthy enough for the prized Secret Service assignment, but Seth could see it in the other man's eyes. Brian cleared his throat. "You're a good fit for us, Anderson. You have a lot of experience with counterfeiting cases, and I don't have time to review all of them." He tossed several more folders onto the pile. "Here are the new ones. Let me know if anything jumps out at you."

"Will do."

Seth closed his eyes as Carlson walked away. The supervisor was hinting that he'd be a permanent part of this group.

Seth dropped the folders on the floor and pushed away from the desk. No way was he going to sit in a cubicle for the rest of his life, dying inch by inch. He'd made it this far. He'd make it back to the protection detail no matter what it took.

Following a brutal two-hour physical therapy session, Seth limped back into his office and eased into his chair. He grimaced as he realized someone had picked up the files and stacked them neatly on his desk. He might not like the pity he saw in everyone's eyes, but he was glad he didn't have to get the folders off the floor. He wasn't sure he'd have made it.

He reached for the top file and scanned it. There was nothing special about the case. Nothing the field agents couldn't handle.

He'd dismissed the other four cases that Carlson had just given him and was ready to toss the last folder on the pile when he saw the name of the town.

Sturgeon Falls, Wisconsin.

His hand tightened. He wasn't certain, but he thought that was where his so-called daughter was living. He'd gotten a letter from an adoption agency, right before he'd been injured, telling him he'd been named the father of a kid. Someone was adopting the girl. The adoption agency would be sending him more information.

Seth hadn't heard anything more before the gunshot that had destroyed his leg and his career. And he sure as hell hadn't been thinking about it while he'd been lying in a bed at Bethesda Naval Hospital.

"What are you still doing here, man? It's five thirty." The young man in the cubicle next to his leaned over the partition. "Need some help getting your stuff to your car?"

"I've got it," Seth said. "But thanks."

Seth stood up and shoved the file into his briefcase. Slinging the bag over his shoulder, he headed down the corridor, trying his hardest not to limp.

By the time he walked into his apartment, his leg was on fire. Pouring himself a glass of scotch, he eyed the pile of mail he'd ignored since he'd gotten home from the hospital. The follow-up letter from the adoption agency must be somewhere in that mess. Finally, with a groan, he began sorting through it.

He found it at the bottom of the stack. The return address was an adoption agency in Sturgeon Falls, Wisconsin. The papers looked genuine. They wanted him to sign away parental rights for a girl named

Regan Sloane. Her mother, a woman named Holly Sloane, had already signed away her rights and had asked that Katriona Macauley adopt the child.

Who the hell was Holly Sloane? Why had she named him as the father? And why did she want this Macauley woman to adopt her kid?

He picked up the phone and called the adoption agency, but he got a recording reciting their office hours and a number to call for emergencies. As he slid the phone back into his pocket, he stared at the papers with a frisson of unease.

He didn't remember dating anyone named Holly Sloane. And he *never* had unprotected sex. So why had this woman claimed he was the father of her child?

He fumbled in his briefcase for the folder he'd brought home and scanned the information. Counterfeit hundred dollar bills had started showing up in Door County, Wisconsin. There had been one or two found in a number of different stores, but the bulk of them had come from a doctor's office in Sturgeon Falls. He stilled when he saw the name of the doctor.

Katriona Macauley.

The same woman who wanted to adopt this girl.

Was it part of some bizarre scheme to hide Macauley's involvement in the counterfeiting? Had she known he was a Secret Service agent? Was that why Holly Sloane had named him as the father?

What was going on? What was the connection?

There had to be one. As far as Seth was concerned, there was no such thing as coincidence. Two things connecting him to a tiny town in northern Wisconsin was one too many to be believed.

Seth pulled out his phone again and pressed a button. "Brian, this is Anderson," he said when he got voice mail. "I've found something interesting with this case in Wisconsin. I think it needs a little undercover work, and it turns out I'm the perfect guy to do it."

Sturgeon Falls, Wisconsin

"IT'S OKAY, BABY," KAT CROONED, sitting in the front seat of her car, rocking a crying Regan in her arms. Wind whipped the pewter clouds above her house into a churning mass and the rain started again. "Grandpa Gus and Grandma Frances will come to Grandparent's Day at your school. Okay?"

"They're not my real grandparents," Regan said, hiccuping around a sob.

Kat brushed the tears away, then kissed her damp, warm cheek. "Your real grandma and grandpa are in heaven with your mom. Do you want to look at the pictures of them?"

"No. I want a real grandma and grandpa like Ellen

and Ginny. How come other kids have real grandparents and I don't?"

Because life isn't fair. "God wanted your mom and grandma and grandpa to be with him. He needed them."

"I need them more."

"I know." She kissed Regan again, then slid her onto the seat of the car. "Let's go into the house. It's going to rain again."

Regan grabbed her backpack and got out of the car. Kat ran to the door of the house and unlocked it, then opened it for Regan. But she was crouched on the sidewalk, peering at a worm.

"What are you doing, honey?" Kat asked.

"There are worms on the sidewalk," Regan answered.

"I know. They come out when it rains."

"I have to move them," Regan said. "They'll die if they stay on the sidewalk."

"Who told you that?"

"One of the boys in my class. He brought a worm into show-and-tell. He knew all about worms."

Regan picked up the worm and carried it to the middle of the lawn. Then she picked up another one and moved it, too. The rain started to fall harder.

"We need to get inside or we're going to get soaked," Kat said.

"I need to move all the worms first." Regan's eyes were dark with worry. "I don't want them to die."

Kat's heart constricted and she bit her lip, her tears blending with the rain. "I'll help you, honey," she said, moving to crouch next to Regan. "Show me how I should pick them up."

By the time she'd gotten Regan to sleep that evening, Kat was exhausted. She glanced at the stack of patient records waiting for her. There was at least an hour of work in that pile of folders. Work she had to finish tonight.

Because tomorrow she'd have another stack of files to write up.

Instead of sitting down and digging in, she headed into the kitchen and poured herself a glass of wine. It had been a rough day.

She'd sent one frightened mother and her young son to the hospital for blood tests. The woman's face had become more pinched, more terrified as Kat had explained the possible causes of her child's recurring tonsillitis.

Another young patient had gone to the hospital with a broken arm, an injury that had been accompanied by bruises on her back and leg. Bruises that hadn't looked accidental to Kat. She'd left a message for Sheriff Godfrey, and he'd be by to talk to her in the morning.

And then Regan had left school with the note about Grandparent's Day.

Sinking into her desk chair, Kat took a drink of the red wine and closed her eyes. As a family-practice physician, she'd treated plenty of parents and their children. She'd been confident that she knew all about the bond between parent and child, understood what being a parent meant.

She'd understood nothing.

She'd told Holly that she loved Regan, promised that she'd take good care of her. But she'd had no idea what love meant. The word was far too weak to describe the fierce, all-consuming emotion she felt for Regan now. And she was terrified that she was failing Regan. Not giving her what she needed. Not knowing the right thing to say or do.

Not able to fill the empty spaces in the child's heart.

Both she and Regan had been seeing a therapist. But Kat still felt completely inadequate. What did she know about being a parent? Especially to a grieving child. She felt as if she were fumbling through each day, making mistakes. Hurting the child she adored.

After taking another sip of wine, she set the glass aside and tried to set her fears aside as well. She had work to do. She used to write up her records at her office, staying late, savoring the quiet after everyone had gone home. Now, in order to pick up Regan at a reasonable time, she brought the files home with her and dealt with them after Regan was in bed.

She needed to sleep herself, but instead she opened the first folder. After a moment, she picked up her pen and began writing.

She'd closed the last file and poured herself another glass of wine when she heard the crunch of footsteps on the gravel driveway. Setting the wine on the coffee table, she slid back the curtain and peered out the window.

A man was walking slowly up the drive, a man she didn't recognize. Probably selling something, she thought with a grimace of irritation. She didn't want to deal with any salesmen tonight.

But as she watched him, the woman in her couldn't help the flash of appreciation. He was tall and rangy, with a face that was tough rather than handsome.

As he got closer, she noticed that he moved too carefully. Stiff, as if in pain. The physician in her watched with sudden interest. Had he recently been injured?

It didn't matter, she thought impatiently. The mother in her was too tired to deal with a salesman. She wouldn't even answer the door.

As she turned away, he stopped and glanced at the front door. Then he looked down at something in his hand.

He was checking her address. Unease slid through her. Door-to-door solicitors didn't check addresses before they approached a house. Clearly, this man was looking for her specifically.

He rang the doorbell, and she studied him for a moment through the peephole. When he stared back, she realized that he'd seen her looking.

She opened the door and made sure the screen door was locked. "Can I help you?"

The man studied her with dark brown eyes, his gaze intense and focused, and she felt a chill. "Are you Katriona Macauley?"

"Yes. Who are you?"

"I'm Seth Anderson. I'm looking for my daughter."

CHAPTER TWO

"WHAT?" KAT GRIPPED THE HANDLE of the screen door. "You can't be Seth Anderson."

His eyebrows rose. "Why not?"

Because Holly liked charmers, slick and superficial guys she could laugh and joke with. Guys she could control. Kat doubted anyone had ever controlled the man in front of her. "You're not Holly's type."

"Appearances can be deceiving." His jaw was set and his gaze drilled into her like a laser.

"Not that deceiving." Holly would never have gotten involved with a man like this. She would have been intimidated by his intensity.

His mouth thinned. He pulled a wallet out of his pocket and flipped it open, held it up to the screen. One side held a gold star that said United States Secret Service, the other an identification card that said he was Seth Anderson. The picture on the card bore only a slight resemblance to the man who stood in front of her. The man on the ID card was the man in the pictures with Holly, a man with a fuller face, a relaxed mouth. A man who might actually smile sometimes.

The man in front of her was gaunt and grim, with lines on his face that weren't in either picture. He looked as if he hadn't smiled in a long time.

When she raised her eyes, he said, "Satisfied?"

Not by a long shot. "What do you want?"

"I want to see this child you claim is my daughter."

His daughter. The words sent a chill through Kat and her belly jumped. "You expect me to let you into my house? At nine o'clock at night?" Kat tightened her grip on the door. "Are you out of your mind?"

As she began to close the door, he said, "Wait. I need to talk to you."

"I'm calling the police," she answered. "If you're really a Secret Service agent, you can prove it to them."

After the door clicked shut and the lock engaged, Kat took a deep, jagged breath. Her hands shook as she punched in the numbers for the sheriff's department.

Five minutes later she heard the siren approaching on County Road TT. Anderson, if that was who he was, leaned against the railing on her front porch, waiting. When Brady Morgan walked up the stairs, she threw open the door.

"What's the problem, Kat?" Brady asked.

"This man showed up and claimed to be a Secret Service agent. He wanted to come into the house."

Brady rested his right hand on his gun and turned to Anderson. "Can I see your ID, please?"

Without a word, Anderson pulled out the same wallet he'd shown her. Brady studied it for a moment, then said, "I'm going to have you sit in my car while I call this in."

"Sure."

Kat watched as the two men headed toward Brady's cruiser. *This can't be happening.* The adoption agency had sent Seth Anderson letters over five months ago. They had clearly stated that if he didn't sign and return the documents or contact the agency, the adoption would be finalized in six months. He'd done neither. Now he showed up just weeks before the adoption was going to be final. What did he want?

She watched as Brady spoke into his radio, talked to Seth Anderson. Finally Brady returned to the door. Anderson trailed behind him, walking more slowly. "He's legit, Kat," Brady said. "We called the Secret Service in Washington and they confirmed he's Seth Anderson and he's one of their agents. They said he's here on personal business."

"Okay." She glanced at Anderson.

"That doesn't mean you have to let him into your house. I just came on duty and I'll be on duty until nine tomorrow morning," Brady said in a low voice. "If you have any problems, you give me a call. Okay?"

"Thanks, Brady." She relaxed a little. "I will."

Brady glanced at the agent as he headed down the steps. "I don't care who you are. Kat doesn't have to talk to you," he said.

As the sheriff's cruiser pulled away, Anderson reached the top of the steps. "I was too abrupt," he said. "I apologize."

"You're in law enforcement. Don't you know better than to show up at a woman's front door at night and try to get into the house?"

"Of course I do. But it's been a long day." He scowled. "I would have been here a lot sooner, but my plane into Milwaukee was delayed and I got stuck in traffic on the drive up here." He sighed. "I just want to meet this girl. Is that so hard to understand?"

No, it wasn't. She'd want the same thing, if she stood in his shoes. "Regan is asleep. And I don't care if Brady vouched for you. You're still not coming into my house."

"Your adoption agency wrote to me, asking me to sign away my parental rights. Did you expect me to do that without asking any questions?"

Kat studied the man on the other side of the door. She read determination in every line of his face. He wasn't going to go away easily. "I thought it was only a formality," she finally said. "I didn't expect you to actually show up."

"You didn't think I'd care when someone tells me I have a child?"

"The agency sent two letters almost six months ago."

"I just got them," he said.

She narrowed her eyes. "They sent them priority mail and I tracked them. Those letters were delivered two days after they were put in the mail."

He clenched his jaw. "I didn't see them until last Friday."

"How come?"

Silence stretched between them. Finally he said, "It doesn't matter. I came as quickly as I could."

"Why didn't you call me before you made a trip here?" Prepare her for the shock. Give her time to muster her defenses.

His eyebrows rose. "What difference would a phone call have made? I was told I have a child. Did you expect me to say 'Oh, that's nice,' and sign the form without checking it out? Without checking *you* out? I want some answers, and some explanations, before I sign away my parental rights."

"You can have all the answers you want. But you're not going to get them tonight." Kat felt her temper rising and struggled to rein it in. She had to stay calm. To think clearly. For Regan's sake.

And her own.

"It's late, Mr. Anderson, and I won't discuss this with you now. Here." She gave him a tight smile. "I have a child to protect, and I don't want her to overhear us. This will have to wait until tomorrow."

She'd meet him somewhere else. Away from Regan.

"Are you trying to hide something?" he asked, his gaze probing. Looking for a weakness.

"I'm not trying to hide a thing. I'm trying to protect my child." Kat stared him down. "And she *is* my child, whether it's legal yet or not. It's what Holly wanted."

"I don't know Holly Sloane." His voice was cold and implacable. "So you can understand why I'm skeptical."

"You can be as skeptical as you want. That's not going to change the truth." Kat took a deep breath and tried again to compose herself. "If you don't think she's yours, you shouldn't have any problem signing the papers to relinquish your rights."

"Kat?" Regan's voice, sleepy and scared, came from behind her. "Why are you yelling?"

Kat snatched the child into her arms, holding her tight and pressing a kiss to her hair. "I'm sorry I woke you up, pumpkin." Without looking at Seth Anderson, she eased the door closed.

"What's wrong?" Regan raised her head and studied Kat's face. Her mouth trembled and her eyes filled with fear. "Why are you mad?"

"I'm not mad, honey," Kat said, carrying her into her bedroom. "I was talking to someone and I got too loud."

"I didn't like that voice," Regan said, her own voice trembling.

"I know, and I'm sorry." She forced herself to relax and smile. "Your teacher would tell me to use my indoor voice, wouldn't she?"

Regan nodded. "Mrs. Stone would have been scared by that yelling."

Kat tucked the covers around Regan. "There's nothing to be scared of," she murmured. "I'm right here. Okay?"

"Okay." She turned to leave, and Regan reached for her. "Stay with me."

Kat sat on the bed, holding Regan's hand, watching her eyes get heavier. When she was sure the girl was asleep, she walked back into the living room, closing the bedroom door behind her.

She stared at the front door. Would Seth Anderson still be standing there? Or would he have given up and gone away.

From what she'd seen so far, there was absolutely no chance he'd given up.

She pulled open the door and found him resting against the railing. He straightened slowly, and she saw a flicker in his eyes that could have been pain. "I apologize if I woke her."

Honesty compelled Kat to say, "I'm afraid I'm the one who woke her up. But clearly this isn't the time or place to have this discussion." She reached over to her desk and picked up a pad of paper. "Give me your cell phone number and I'll call you tomorrow when I know what my schedule is like. I'll get a babysitter and meet you in the evening."

He recited his number, then raised his eyebrows. "Why don't you bring her with you? Don't you think I have the right to meet her?"

"I have no proof that you're her father, other than the words of a dying woman. And you don't remember Holly." She studied his face with a surge of hope. Regan looked nothing like him. "Maybe she's not yours."

"I'm not going to leave without being sure," Seth said, gentling his tone. "Is that so hard to understand?"

No. If their positions were reversed, she'd want to know, as well. Want to meet Regan. Want to know whether or not she had a child.

Even though it was the right thing to do, she still hesitated. "All right," she said reluctantly. "I'll bring her with me. But you can't even hint that you're her father. If it's true, if you are Regan's father, *I'll* decide if and when to tell her."

He watched her for a moment, his eyes hard and

unyielding. Finally he nodded. "Fine. But I'm going to have a DNA test done tomorrow. I expect you to test the girl, as well."

"She's already been tested." She'd tested Regan as soon as the adoption agency had sent the letter to Seth Anderson, and the results were tucked away in her desk. A ticking time bomb, counting down the minutes until detonation.

"You're a physician, aren't you? Can you do the test?"

"How do you know I'm a physician?"

He smiled, but it didn't extend to his eyes. "I did background checks on you and Holly Sloane. I wanted to know who you were."

"Isn't that abuse of power?" She didn't like knowing he had browsed through the details of her life. Or Holly's.

"The private investigator that your adoption agency hired did the same thing to me. I just cut out the middleman."

"All right. Come to my office tomorrow. I'll call in a favor and get the results stat."

He regarded her coolly. "Something about that bothers me. Maybe it would be best if I went to an independent lab."

"Fine." Her hand tightened on the door. "Let me know what lab you choose and I'll send Regan's results there." Without waiting for an answer, she closed the door.

She watched through the curtained front window as he descended the steps, then limped heavily back to his car.

Guilt spread through her. He *had* been injured. And she'd made him stand on the porch, in the cold damp of an October night, for far too long.

It had been his choice to come here tonight, she reminded herself. His choice to stand on her porch.

Only a very determined man would have stayed on her porch, would have waited her out in spite of his obvious pain. Why? What did he want?

Did he want Regan?

Fear trailed after her as she turned off the lights and put on her pajamas. It slid into bed alongside her and haunted her dreams.

Regan was hers, had been hers since the day they'd stood side by side and watched Holly lowered into the ground. This man who didn't even remember Regan's mother had no claim on the little girl.

Except, possibly, the claim of blood.

LATE THE NEXT MORNING, Barbara Morris, Kat's receptionist, stuck her head in the office door. "Patient in room A, Kat." She wiggled her eyebrows. "He's a hottie."

"Tall, dark and handsome?" Kat said with a grin.

"Oh, yeah. And friendly, too. A real charmer. If I wasn't deliriously happy with Craig, I might try my luck."

Kat stood up. "Then I'd better get in there and save you from yourself." She reached for the folder on the exam-room door and flipped it open.

Froze. It was Seth Anderson.

He'd come for the test after all.

And he was Barb's charming hottie? Could they possibly be talking about the same man?

Gathering her composure, she touched the stethoscope curled in her pocket, reminding herself she was in charge here. Then she straightened her lab coat and opened the door.

Seth was sitting in the chair, massaging his right thigh. When she stepped into the room, he shifted in the chair and slid his hand into his pocket. The move was so smooth and fast that she suspected he'd used it frequently. To hide the fact that his leg hurt.

"Good morning, Mr. Anderson. You changed your mind about me doing the paternity test?"

Dull red splashed his cheeks. "It makes sense for you to do it. I was rude last night. My only excuse is that I was tired." He glanced at his leg. "It had been a long day."

"What's wrong with your leg?" she asked in a professional tone. "Anything I can help you with?"

"No. Thank you. My leg is fine." As if to prove it, he stretched his legs out in front of him. "Just do the test, and I'll get out of your hair."

She picked up the needle and blood collection tube that Barb had set on the counter for her. "Since I already tested Regan, once I have your sample, it should only take a few days to get the results."

Now that she saw Seth Anderson up close and in the light, she saw a resemblance to Regan. Her hair color was different than Seth's, and so was her eye color. But there were similarities in the shapes of their faces. Regan's chin had the same stubborn attitude as Seth's. And the curve of Seth's mouth mirrored Regan's when the girl was determined.

Kat picked up the tubes and the needle. Her hands shaking, she fitted the needle into the holder and slid the tube into place, then lifted his arm. His warm skin was dusted with dark hair and smelled like the medicinal soap found in cheap motels.

When she tied the tourniquet, his ropy muscles tensed.

"Can you relax your arm a bit?" she asked, her voice gentle. "It will make this easier for both of us."

"Sorry." Clenching his jaw, he relaxed his fist and shifted in the chair. "Go ahead."

His muscles weren't as tense, but his vein was a hard, tight band beneath his skin, thick with scar tissue. She stared at it for a moment. Seth Anderson had had a lot of blood samples drawn. Recently. "It's going to be difficult to find your vein in this arm," she said, unfastening the tourniquet. "Let me see your other arm."

"That one is worse," he said.

She waited for an explanation, but Seth didn't say a thing. Finally she asked, "Do you want me to try, or just do a cheek swab? A swab would take longer to get the results."

"Do the swab," he said.

Discarding the needle, she took a swab in a plastic tube out of the drawer, along with a tongue depressor. "Open your mouth, please."

He smelled like coffee, with a faint, underlying scent of mint toothpaste. The familiar, homey smells made her freeze in the act of rubbing the swab over the inside of his mouth.

He wasn't the embodiment of evil, someone who'd come to take her daughter away from her. He was just a man, someone who'd had coffee this morning and brushed his teeth.

Taking a deep breath, she stepped away from him.

She scribbled on the chart and filled out the billing form, then opened the door. As she handed the file to Annie Smith, her nurse, she gave Seth a strained smile. "I'll see you this evening. If we meet at a playground, Regan can climb on the equipment while we talk. Will six o'clock work for you?"

He nodded. "I'll see you then."

Kat felt Barb's gaze on her. As soon as Seth left the office, Barb hooted. "My God," she said, admiration in her eyes. "You're a fast worker. You already set up a date with Mr. McHottie?"

"'Mr. McHottie?'" Kat forced herself to smile back. "This is the guy you were talking about? The charmer who was so friendly? Are you sure we're talking about the same guy? Because he wasn't real charming or friendly in the exam room."

"Probably scared of needles," Annie piped up. "Doesn't that make you go all protective?"

"Nope. I don't go for wimps." What would Barb and Annie think if Kat told them Seth Anderson was the least wimpy guy she knew?

"That didn't stop you from making a date with him, did it?" With a sly smile, Barb said, "I guess sexy covers a multitude of sins."

"I'm shocked, Barb." Kat kept forcing a smile onto her face. "Is a mother allowed to say things like that? I hope you don't talk that way around Randy."

The smile on Barb's face dimmed. "No, Randy and I mostly talk about his falling grades and his poor choice of friends."

"I'm sorry." Shaking her head, berating herself for her insensitivity, Kat leaned forward and touched her receptionist's hand. "I need to think before I talk."

"Don't worry about it, Kat. I'm not that sensitive." Barb snorted. "How can I be? It's been going on ever since the divorce."

"It's not getting any better?" Kat asked, glad to have the subject of Seth Anderson off the table.

"No." Barb's lips tightened. "First he was angry that I'm seeing Craig. Now he's sneaking around, not coming home when he's supposed to, not telling me where he's been."

"I think a lot of boys have trouble with their mother dating after a divorce," Kat said.

"Not just boys," Annie chimed in. "Hayley wasn't happy when Dylan started dating Charlotte, either."

Barb shook her head. "It's not that, or at least not completely. Jealousy I could deal with. Randy seems to hate Craig. He calls Craig the jerkosaurus, and that's when he's in a good mood. He makes it a point to stay in the room with us whenever Craig is at the house."

"He's a teenager," Annie said. "Dating gets really complicated with a teen in the house." She grimaced. "Thank goodness Hayley decided she liked Charlotte. I think I'm going to wait until she's in college before I date anyone."

"Come on, guys," Kat said with a smile. "You're

scaring me. A lot. Regan is only six. I don't want to wait twelve more years before I have another date."

"Doesn't sound like you'll have to," Barb said with a grin. "You're seeing Mr. Anderson tonight."

"It's business," Kat said.

"That's better than nothing," Annie retorted. "The only hot guy I've spent any time with recently is the deputy who gave me a speeding ticket this morning."

"Ouch," Kat said lightly. "That bites."

"You know it," Annie said. "Now, even if I see Brady Morgan again, I'll be too embarrassed to talk to him."

"Brady gave you a ticket?" Kat shook her head with a smile, relieved they'd gotten off the subject of Seth Anderson. "I went to high school with him, and I thought he was brighter than that. I'll be sure to tell him that he just wrecked his chances with you."

Annie rolled her eyes. "Like he would re-member me."

"Don't sell yourself short, Annie," Kat said, escaping into her office. She closed the door before Annie or Barb asked anything more about her "date" with Seth. She didn't want to tell them who Seth was, at least not yet.

That would mean she'd have to admit it to herself.

CHAPTER THREE

SETH ANDERSON SAT ON A BENCH near the playground at Sunset Park, willing himself to ignore the aching muscles in his right leg. The sky was leaden and gray, and a damp wind sliced through the thin jacket he wore. But he'd told Katriona Macauley he'd meet her, so here he'd stay. Even if the damp chill was making his leg hurt like a son of a bitch.

She was late. Glancing at his watch again, he wondered if she'd changed her mind. Had she balked at meeting him? Rethought whatever scheme she had cooking?

The two women who worked in her office didn't look like criminals. They'd been normal and pleasant. Average. Nothing suspicious about them, at least not on the surface.

Katriona Macauley didn't seem like the counterfeiting type, either. But he'd learned not to make quick judgments.

They could get you killed.

He shifted on the bench, trying to find a more comfortable position, and smiled grimly. If the doctor thought he'd go away just because she threw up a few roadblocks, she'd seriously underestimated him. He was determined to get to the bottom of this counterfeiting case.

And if Macauley was behind it, she'd end up in prison, where she belonged.

But what about the kid?

If the kid was his, he'd do the right thing. He'd make sure she was taken care of. He'd been a foster child, shunted from family to family until he'd escaped at eighteen, and no child of his would suffer that way.

He stood up and walked around the playground, trying to shake out the stiffness in his leg. He'd circled the playground for a second time before he saw car lights in the parking lot.

The doors slammed and a woman and child began walking across the field toward him. The child was plastered against the woman's leg and held tightly to her hand.

He couldn't see the woman clearly, but he knew it was Macauley. He'd known the minute she'd gotten out of the car. It was his job, he told himself. He'd spent his life analyzing body language and body movement. That was why he could tell it was Katriona Macauley who walked toward him.

As the pair stepped under a streetlight, Kat's bright red hair fluttered around her shoulders, a warm and welcoming fire on a cold night. Macauley walked more slowly once she spotted him, and the girl looked up to her. Asking her a question.

Katriona and the girl stopped in front of him, and the child edged closer to the woman. Macauley held his eyes for a long moment, then crouched down. "This is Mr. Anderson, Regan."

Seth bent and offered the girl his hand. "Nice to meet you, Regan," he said.

"Hello," she answered. She didn't offer to shake his hand, but studied him for a long moment with enormous, dark blue eyes. Her dark blond hair was chin length and messy, and her chin had a stubborn set. He saw nothing of himself in her.

He withdrew his hand and stood up, scanning the doctor's eyes. But he didn't see the calculation he expected. He saw caution and a hint of fear, quickly hidden.

"Regan, you can play for a few minutes," Katriona said. She smiled down at the girl. "Then we'll go eat."

"Mackydoos?" Regan asked.

"Yep. Mackydoos."

With a careful glance at him, Regan ran off and climbed onto a wooden tower. Kat watched her and waved.

"Thank you for coming, Dr. Macauley," he said.

"Call me Kat. And you're welcome, but I told you we'd be here." She glanced at her watch and grimaced. "I'm sorry we're late. I got held up at the office."

"Patient emergency?" he asked casually.

"Forms to be filled out for insurance," she said with a sigh. "There's a never-ending stream of them."

"Doesn't anyone pay cash anymore?"

"Some do. But it's mostly insurance claims." She shoved her hands into her coat pockets. "One of these days I might make enough money to hire another person to deal with all the paperwork."

"Something to look forward to." And a motive to pass counterfeit money, he thought grimly. He stretched his leg, trying to ignore the cramp developing in it. "Do you mind if we walk?"

"It's too cold to talk out here," she said, pulling the collar of her woolen coat more tightly around her neck as she paced with him. She glanced at his leg, and he forced himself not to limp. "I'm taking Regan to McDonald's for dinner. Why don't you join us? She can play in their indoor playground and we can talk."

"Are you sure?"

"Yes." She transferred her gaze to him. "We'll both be more comfortable." She glanced down at his leg again and he braced for the pity. He'd had too much of it in the past six months. Instead, when she looked at him, all he saw in her eyes was curiosity.

"Fine," he said, reluctantly impressed. He could handle curiosity. "I'll follow you there."

She called to Regan and the three of them walked toward the parking lot. His rented sedan was next to her small SUV, and he watched as she buckled the girl into a booster seat. Then she slid into the driver's seat and pulled away without looking at him.

AS THEY FINISHED their meal, Seth watched Regan jump into a ball pit in the play area. Red, blue and yellow balls flew into the air as he asked Kat, "When do you expect to get the results of the paternity test?"

She took a sip of iced tea as she watched Regan. "It should take five days or so. I'll let you know as soon as I get the results."

"She doesn't look anything like me," he said.

She studied him, her blue eyes traveling over his face. He knew she saw his suspicion.

"There's a faint resemblance," she said.

"I told you I don't even know a Holly Sloane."

Kat fumbled in her purse and pulled out two Polaroid pictures. "Does this refresh your memory?"

The man smiling out of the photos was him, there was no doubt. Even though that young man bore practically no resemblance to the man he was now.

And the pretty blond woman beside him looked vaguely familiar. Uneasiness slid through him. "That's me."

"And Holly. You look pretty friendly."

"Where was this taken? And when?"

"In Milwaukee. Seven years ago this month."

He did remember the woman. He'd been amazed she'd chosen him over all the pretty college boys in the bar that night. "I used a condom," he said.

"You remember Holly?"

"Yes. I don't usually have one-night stands."

"Why that night?"

He stared out the window at the darkness. "I was lonely. I think she was, too."

"Yes." Kat moved her cup of iced tea, turning it so the logo faced front. "She had graduated the spring before and was missing school, missing her friends. She was visiting me, but I had an early class the next day. She wasn't ready to call it a night, so she stayed at the bar after I left. I guess that's when she hooked up with you."

"Are you blaming yourself?" he asked, incredulous.

She shrugged. "Partly. If I hadn't gone back to my apartment, Holly might not have been lonely."

"And we might not have met."

"Who knows? But she wasn't sorry." Kat smiled and her eyes went soft. "At first she was terrified—

she was only twenty-two, and she didn't know how she was going to support herself and a baby. But Holly grew up fast. She found a good job and was an incredible mother. She and Regan were happy together."

"What happened to Holly?"

"She had cancer. She passed away in April."

"Maybe she was wrong about me." He hesitated, unsure how to phrase it. "Maybe it was someone else who got her pregnant."

"She was sure it was you." The softness disappeared. "She searched for you for over a year. She only gave up when the P.I. she hired told her he'd run out of leads."

His unease slid into worry. He'd gone into the Secret Service not long after their encounter. He wasn't surprised she hadn't been able to find him. He hadn't left a very big trail.

"There's very little chance that Regan is my daughter," he said. "A one-night stand, condoms…" He shrugged. "The odds are against it."

He looked into the play area and saw the girl. Instead of a grin, like most of the other kids, the girl had a look of fierce resolve on her face as she climbed the red-and-yellow plastic structure. As if she was determined to defeat it.

"Condoms can fail." Kat picked up her drink and took a sip, and her hand wasn't quite steady. "And your name is on Regan's birth certificate. If you're her father, you have to sign away your parental rights so the adoption can go through."

"What if I don't sign? What if she's mine and I want to raise her myself?"

The cup of iced tea spilled on the table. "You can't be serious." She grabbed a handful of napkins and began mopping up the mess.

"How do I know you're a good mother? That you'll take good care of her?"

"I love Regan, Mr. Anderson. I was in the delivery room when she was born. She spent every Christmas with me and my family. Holly moved up here when she was dying so I could help her take care of Regan. She wanted me to raise her child." She looked at the play area, where Regan was at the top of the slide, talking to some other children. "She's my child now."

"The adoption isn't final yet."

Kat shoved the cup away from her. "Are you threatening me, Mr. Anderson?"

Shame burned in his gut. Threatening a mother with the loss of her child was cruel and heartless. But if Kat was his counterfeiter, she didn't deserve to raise Regan. "Why would I threaten you?"

"I have no idea." Kat's gaze probed his, and he finally looked away. "But you're after something. I just haven't figured out what it is."

"I came here to find out if this child is mine. And if she is, I want to make sure you're going to take care of her before I sign away my rights."

"The adoption agency did an exhaustive investigation of me, and they approved the adoption. Do you want money? Is that what you're after? Do you expect me to pay you for your signature on that piece of paper?" Kat's face was flushed and her blue eyes sparked.

"Of course not." He stared at her, shocked. "You think I'd sell a child?"

"I don't know you. I have no idea what you'd do."

"I don't sell children, that's for damn sure." He felt his face heat. "Is it so hard to believe I'd care about what happened to my own flesh and blood?"

"It took you long enough to decide you cared," she snapped. "Why did it take you so long to open that letter from the adoption agency?"

He instinctively reached for his leg, then caught himself and curled his hand into a fist. "I was away," he said after a pause. "I wasn't getting my mail."

"You let your mail pile up for six months?" She raised her eyebrows. "That's pretty irresponsible."

"The reason I couldn't come earlier isn't important," he said. "I'm here now, and I'm determined to do the right thing."

"And what *is* the right thing, as far as you're concerned?" Kat leaned across the table, holding his eyes with hers. "Do you think you're going to take her away from me, raise her yourself?"

"I never thought about having children. But if she's mine and if I decide you're not the right person to raise her, then yes. If necessary, I'll raise her myself."

Kat stood up so abruptly her chair toppled over. "I'll call you when I get the results of the paternity test," she said. "Until then, don't try to contact me and don't come near Regan. Secret Service agent or not, I'll call the police in a heartbeat if I think you're threatening my child."

She headed toward the play area and he stood slowly, cursing the injury that had stolen his mobility and quickness. "Kat, wait."

She stopped. After a moment, she turned, anger burning in her eyes. Seth felt the other patrons watching him, but he ignored them as he limped toward Kat. "What's the problem? I thought we were having a conversation."

"A *conversation*? I don't think so. You've known Regan for about an hour. You're a complete stranger to her. She hasn't recovered from her mother's death and now you're going to take her away from everything familiar to her? You tell me this then you ask what the problem is?" She glared at him with scornful eyes. "What planet are you from, Mr. Anderson?"

"I guess that would be the planet Clueless." He knew enough about women to realize he needed to retreat. "I'm not judging you, Kat. I don't know anything about you. I'm just being logical. I'm trying to cover all the bases."

She narrowed her eyes. "Fine. You're logical and I'm pissed off. In the five days until the paternity test comes back, you can try to be a little less logical and I can try to be a little less pissed off. Maybe then we can have an actual conversation."

She headed into the play area and corralled Regan. Seth watched Kat frown as she listened to the girl, who was talking and pointing at the play structure. Kat looked around, but Regan shook her head. Kat squatted to help the girl put on her shoes, and as she talked to Regan, warmth softened Kat's eyes, enveloping Regan. Surrounding her with love.

The frozen places inside of him yearned for that kind of warmth. For the past six months, he'd lived in a cold world of pain and despair and isolation. A colorless, sterile world. He'd forgotten there was anything else.

Before he could leave, Kat ushered Regan through the door and saw him. "I thought you were leaving, Mr. Anderson," she said casually.

"I'll walk you and Regan to your car," he answered. He glanced down at the girl, who was walking close to Kat. "You looked like you were having a good time in there, Regan."

She nodded. "I climbed all the way to the top."

"I saw you," he said, wondering how he was supposed to respond. He had no idea how to talk to a kid.

"Some big boys pushed me and told me to get lost. They said it was their fort."

"Someone pushed you?" He surveyed the play area. "Who was it?"

"They're not here anymore. I told them they couldn't make me. They pushed me again, and I pushed them back. So they went down the slide and didn't come back."

"That's good." He looked at Kat. "Isn't it?"

Kat smoothed her hand over Regan's hair. "Regan promised that if this happens again, she'll come and get me and I'll handle the situation," she said. She smiled at the girl. "Adults are supposed to handle bullies."

"But you stood up for yourself," he said to Regan.

Kat picked the girl up and hugged her. "She could have gotten hurt."

At the car, Kat buckled Regan into her car seat and closed the door. When she straightened, her eyes flashed. "What's the matter with you, telling her it was all right to push those boys? Do you want her to think she did the right thing?"

"Maybe she did. There's not always an adult who can help you. Sometimes you have to help yourself."

"Regan has me to help her."

"You're always going to be there when she needs you?"

"No," she said quietly. "Of course not. I wasn't there when she needed me tonight, was I? But there has to be a better way than pushing back." She studied his eyes, and he looked away before she could see too much.

"Sometimes, there's not."

"It sounds as if you don't have a lot of faith in people, Agent."

He shrugged. "This isn't about me."

"Isn't it?" Kat slid into the front seat of her car. "I'll call you when I get the results of the test."

He watched until the car disappeared down the highway, the taillights blending with all the other cars on the road. Then he limped to his rental car.

He didn't have a clue about raising kids. Whether Macauley was guilty or not, what the hell was he going to do if the girl really *was* his?

CHAPTER FOUR

KAT'S EYES BURNED as she stared at the file in front of her. The words blurred together and the note Annie had attached to the folder didn't make any sense.

Frustrated, she tossed the file onto her desk and rubbed her eyes. It was her own fault, she told herself. Seth Anderson had pushed all her buttons. Even worse, she'd let him. No wonder she hadn't slept last night.

Shoving away from the desk, she took the folder to the front desk. Before she could ask Annie what the note meant, the door to the office flew open and Barb's son, Randy, slouched in. White earbuds protruded from his ears and his head bobbed to the music.

"Hi, Randy," she said.

"Hey, Dr. Mac," he muttered, pulling the earbuds out. The teen hitched up his baggy jeans and scanned the room. When he saw his mother behind the counter, he sauntered over to her. "I brought you a cup of coffee," he told Barb, setting it down carefully.

"Thanks, Randy." Barb looked astonished as she took a sip. "That was very thoughtful of you."

"Whatever." He peered around the corner of the desk. "Isn't Jenna working today?"

"Ah." Barb hid her grin behind the coffee cup. "She's in the back, running off some copies."

Randy attempted nonchalance. "Is it okay if I go back there to say hi to her?" he asked.

Barb glanced at Kat, who struggled to look properly serious. She didn't want Randy to think she was laughing at him. She remembered too well the anxiety and drama of high-school crushes. "Sure. Go ahead."

Randy disappeared around the corner, and Kat heard him talking in a low voice to the girl who worked after school, doing the filing. She smiled at Barb. "Isn't that the third time this week?"

Barb rolled her eyes. "It's amazing how, all of a sudden, Mr.-Independent-I'm-sixteen-years-old-so-don't-bug-me wants to see his dear old mom after school." She took another sip of the coffee and grimaced. "Where on earth did he get this? It tastes like it was scraped off a floor." She set the cup down with a shudder.

"All these after-school visits are because of Jenna?" Kat asked.

"Apparently." She touched the coffee cup. "He's supposed to call me when he gets home so I know he's there." She glanced over her shoulder toward Randy's voice. "He's not stopping here because he's so eager to see me, that's for sure."

"I think it's sweet," Annie said. Her curly brown hair floated around her shoulders as she leaned backward, trying to see past the shelves of patient files to where Randy had disappeared. "Maybe he'll straighten himself out if he's trying to impress Jenna."

"Please." Barb shook her head. "That just brings up a whole new set of problems. He doesn't want to hear the sex lecture from me, and his father sure isn't a shining example of responsibility."

"Thank goodness I don't have to worry about that for a long time," Kat said fervently.

Annie snickered. "Yeah, you only have to worry about yourself."

"Not lately, I don't," Kat said, her voice dry.

"That's not what it looks like from the cheap seats." Barb wriggled her eyebrows. "How was your date with the hottie last night?"

"You mean Mr. Anderson?" Kat shook her head. "We didn't have a date."

"Give it up, Kat. We heard you make plans with him. And he was in here again today." Barb smirked. "He paid us for the test you did yesterday. Said he didn't think his insurance company would cover it."

"Seth Anderson was in here today? And you didn't tell me?"

"You weren't here," Barb said.

"I've been here all day."

"He came in over lunch." Barb's grin faded. "While you were at Regan's school. Is there a problem?"

"Of course not," Kat managed to say. "I just didn't expect it." She looked from one of her employees to the other. Both of them avoided her gaze. "What?"

Barb finally said, "He's a nice guy, Kat. We talked for a while, since there weren't any patients. He seems interested in you."

She'd just bet he seemed interested. "So did you give him all the dirt on me?" she asked, keeping her voice light.

"Yeah, we told him about your pitiful lack of dates. We encouraged him to change that."

"Tell me you're joking," Kat said, heat washing over her. "Please."

"Of course we are," Barb said. "We're not going to talk to a stranger about you. Even if he *is* hot. We were very businesslike." She grinned. "I had my matchmaking tendencies firmly under control."

"Thank goodness," Kat muttered.

"We didn't talk about you personally," Annie reassured her. "We were too busy taking his money. We mostly talked about the practice."

"The practice?" Kat looked from Barb to Annie, uneasiness sliding through her. "He asked you about my business?"

"Not exactly." Barb took a sip of coffee and grimaced again. "He paid cash, and we kind of kidded him about it. Told him that no one paid cash anymore."

"And he was interested in that?" Kat looked from Barb to Annie, now puzzled as well as alarmed. He'd asked her something about the practice last night, as well. About cash and insurance.

"Sounded like it." Barb's grin had faded. "Since he paid in cash, I had to go into the lab to put it in the cash box. He asked me why we kept the cash back there, and I told him we didn't want to leave cash at the front desk—too tempting if someone walks in and there's no one at the desk. He asked a couple of questions." She shrugged. "I thought he was just making conversation. Is he an accountant or something?"

"I have no idea." Kat looked from Barb to Annie, wondering if the Secret Service hired accountants like the FBI. "Let me know the next time he shows up, okay?"

"Sure."

Before Kat could ask Annie anything more about Seth's visit to the office, Randy strolled into the reception area. "I'm going home, Ma," he said.

"Call me when you get there," Barb answered.

"Yeah, yeah." Randy slipped out the door, and moments later Jenna appeared. One buckle on her baggy overalls wasn't completely hooked.

"Did you get that filing done?" Barb asked, drilling her with a steely gaze.

"Yes, Mrs. Morris," she answered.

Barb handed her another stack of folders. "Good. Here's some more."

Kat went back into her office, shut the door and leaned against it. Why had Seth come to her office with the lame excuse of paying his bill?

At a time she might not be there.

He was checking up on her. Asking her employees questions about her.

Anger warred with grudging admiration. He was abrasive and abrupt, he seemed cold and distant, but apparently he was serious about making sure Regan was well cared for. She could forgive a lot if it was done out of concern for her child.

Pulling out her phone, she punched in Seth's number. After a few rings, he answered.

"Anderson."

His voice was rough and raspy and already too familiar. "Mr. Anderson, this is Kat Macauley. The next time you want to talk to my employees about me, don't bother with a lame excuse like paying your bill. And wait until after office hours. I don't want my patients to overhear you."

There was a long beat of silence. "Kat," he finally said. "I'm sorry I upset you."

"You're invading my privacy and I don't like it. But I understand your concern about Regan. I would probably do the same thing. Just don't do it behind my back."

"Thank you for permission to snoop," he said dryly. "I appreciate it."

"I'll do anything I have to do for Regan," Kat said, ignoring the tiny frisson of awareness. "I'll call you when I have the test results." Without waiting for an answer, she shut her phone.

What kind of man said he didn't want children, knew nothing about them, but flew almost a thousand miles to make sure a child was in good hands? A child he didn't even think was his.

An honorable one, she realized reluctantly. A man who was determined to do the right thing, no matter the cost. Seth could have just signed the papers and not given Regan another thought. Instead, he'd gone far out of his way to make sure she was in good hands.

She didn't have to like Seth Anderson, but she had to respect him.

"THIS GOES NO FARTHER THAN YOU," Seth warned Sheriff Godfrey. "And one deputy. I don't want to spook anyone. We're going to have to be careful with this counterfeiter."

"I know how to keep my mouth shut," Godfrey answered. He shifted his bulk in the desk chair and shook his head. "But I can't believe Kat Macauley would be involved. I've known her family since before she was born. They're good people. Solid."

"I hope you're right. But since a lot of the money is coming from her practice, she's a suspect."

"The bank is positive it's her money?"

"Yes." Seth stood up and paced the small office. "Whoever is passing it probably thinks they're getting away with it, which is what we want them to think. Kat doesn't know I'm here to investigate her office, and I want to keep it that way."

Godfrey tilted his head. "Why does she think you're here?"

"It's a personal matter between me and Kat. It's not important to the case."

"Okay." Godfrey's chair creaked as he stood up. "I can't take an active role in the investigation." He grimaced. "Someone made a stink about the way we handled a case, and I'm sticking to administrative crap for a while. I'm going to have Brady Morgan work with you. He's young, but he's sharp."

"Good. I appreciate the cooperation, Sheriff." So Godfrey was riding a desk for a while. Seth hoped it wasn't going to affect his investigation.

"Always happy to cooperate with the feds." Godfrey walked to the door and stuck his head out. "Morgan? You out there?"

"Be right there, Sheriff," a voice called. A few moments later, a tall young man with dark blond hair and wide shoulders walked into the room. The deputy who'd come to Kat's door that first night. "You need something, Stan?" he asked the sheriff.

The sheriff nodded at Seth. "This is Agent Seth Anderson from the Secret Service," he said. "Anderson, Brady Morgan."

"We've met," Brady said, assessing Seth.

Seth nodded. "I need your help," he said.

"Is this about the other night? When I called you in?" Brady narrowed his eyes.

"Of course not. You did the right thing. I'm here working a case."

"Involving Kat Macauley?" Seth didn't miss the skepticism in Morgan's voice.

The sheriff headed for the door. "I'll leave you two to discuss it."

After the sheriff closed the door behind himself, Seth leaned against his desk. "Have a seat, Morgan.

I'm here about a counterfeiting case. It involves Dr. Macauley's medical practice."

"Kat?" Brady asked, astonished. "Counterfeiting money?"

"I didn't say it was her. It's going through her practice."

"Maybe one of her patients gave her a phony bill."

"It's happened too many times—three or four times a week for the past few weeks. Each time a single hundred-dollar bill. Some of the other businesses in the area have gotten them, but there hasn't been a pattern like with Macauley."

Brady frowned. "She has people working for her. Just because it came through her office doesn't mean it's Kat."

Seth raised an eyebrow. "You seem pretty sure it's not Macauley. You have a personal stake there?"

"If you're asking if I'm dating Kat, the answer is no." The young man looked out the window, avoiding Seth's gaze. "We went out a couple of times in high school, but we didn't click. We're just friends."

"You know any of the other people who work there?"

"I know Barb Morris. My older sister went to school with her. Barb's son Randy hangs out with a couple of losers, but we haven't had any problems with him. Yet."

"There's another woman named Annie Smith who works there. What about her?"

To Seth's surprise, the deputy's face turned red. "She moved here a couple months ago. I gave her a speeding ticket the other day. I hated to do it, but she was going twenty over the limit. Hard to give her just a warning."

"Why'd you hate to do it?"

Brady grimaced. "Tough to ask a woman out after you've handed her a ninety-dollar speeding ticket."

"You interested in dating her?"

"Yeah. I just haven't gotten up the nerve to ask her."

Seth stood up and paced the office. "Okay. I want you to ask her out. Get to know her. See if she's having any money troubles, anything that would make her likely to pass bad money."

"But…I really like her. I don't want to spy on her."

"If things work out and she hasn't done anything, she never has to know why you started seeing her. If she's guilty?" Seth shrugged. "She's going to prison and you won't be able to date her anyway."

"That's pretty cold," the deputy said.

Seth gave him a smile with no warmth. "I'm not in Sturgeon Falls to make friends, Morgan. I'm here to get a job done. If you're not interested in helping me, I'm sure Sheriff Godfrey can find someone who is."

"No, I'll ask her out. I want to work this case with you."

"Good. And one more thing. You don't tell anyone else what you're doing—not your mother, not your best friend, not your dog. No one."

"I know my job, Anderson."

"Good. We'll meet every couple days to compare notes."

"Are you going to be investigating Kat?"

"Yes."

"You're not going to find anything. She's as straight as they come."

"I hope so, Morgan." If she wasn't, Seth would be responsible for Regan. A kid he knew nothing about.

CHAPTER FIVE

KAT GRIPPED THE PHONE as she stared down at the piece of paper in her hand. "It's Kat Macauley, Mr. Anderson. We need to meet."

"Did you get the test results?" Seth's voice roughened.

"Are you free at noon?"

There was a pause at the other end. She imagined him glancing at his watch, wondering if forty minutes was enough time. Would he look forward to seeing her? Or would he dread it?

She was an idiot. What difference did it make? This was business, and that was all.

"Yes," he said. "Where would you like to meet?"

"My house." It was as private as they could get. She had no intention of discussing this in a public place. "Do you remember how to get there?"

"Yes. I'll see you at noon." He hung up before she could answer.

She dropped the phone into its cradle and rubbed

her damp palms on her white lab coat. Okay, then. Showdown at high noon.

Over Regan.

She saw three more patients before she left, trying to focus on their problems instead of her own. Finally, when the last patient walked out at 11:45, she hurried through the door.

Instead of driving directly home, she drove past Regan's school. The first graders were on the playground, and she pulled over to the curb to watch them.

It wasn't hard to find Regan in her bright pink coat, climbing to the top of the slide, then flying down with a grin. Another little girl came down immediately after Regan, and then the two girls ran toward the ladder again.

Regan was making friends. Her mother had died and her life had changed forever, but the girl was settling into her life with Kat. Relishing the normality of first grade, recess and other children. A routine.

Kat would *not* allow Seth Anderson to rip Regan away from the life Kat was slowly helping her build. She'd do whatever was necessary to prevent him from taking Regan away.

She pulled away from the curb and drove toward her house. The closer she got, the more slowly she drove. When she finally pulled into the driveway, Seth's rented Ford Taurus was already waiting.

Seth saw Kat's small SUV appear around the curve of the road. It looked as if it slowed down as it got closer. It was crawling when it finally turned into the driveway.

He eased out of the car as she slammed the car door and headed for the house. "What's up?" he asked. Although he knew; she'd gotten the test results.

She shook her head as she unlocked her door. He struggled to catch up with her as she stood waiting for him. Once he stepped into the house, she closed the door behind him and tossed her coat on a dining-room chair. Disappearing into the kitchen, she called, "Would you like something to drink?"

"No, thanks," he answered as he wove his way through the toys on the floor to the kitchen. The end tables were piled with books and two stuffed frogs sat on the plaid couch. Several vibrant, impressionistic paintings covered the walls. They were all landscapes, and the vistas looked familiar. Door County?

By the time he reached the kitchen, she'd poured herself a glass of iced tea. She held out the pitcher in his direction. "Sure you don't want some?"

"No. Thank you," he added. "I just want to know what's going on. Did you get the results of the test?"

Kat put the pitcher back into the refrigerator, then turned to face him. "Yes. It came this morning."

"And?"

She set her glass of iced tea down on the counter. Taking a paper out of the pocket of her slacks, she unfolded it and offered it to him.

"You're her biological father."

It wasn't possible. He'd convinced himself that Holly had made a mistake. That the test would come back negative and he'd put the issue behind him. Then he'd be able to investigate the counterfeiting case without any troubling personal connections.

She pushed the paper closer to him, and he reluctantly took it.

He had a child. Regan was his flesh and blood. How was he supposed to feel? Happy? Proud? Was he supposed to instantly love the kid?

The only thing he felt was fear.

No. Fear wasn't in his emotional repertoire. It wasn't allowed.

It was a puzzle. Something he had to figure out. Nothing more.

He focused on the graphs and words in front of him. "The margin of error on these tests is about three billion to one, if it's done properly. Is this lab reliable?"

"Sorry to disappoint you, but yes. They're extremely reliable." Kat's voice sharpened. "I don't send my lab work to fly-by-night outfits. They're one of the oldest and most respected labs in Wisconsin."

"Did they run it twice?" he asked. "To make sure there wasn't any contamination?"

"Yes." She pointed to the graphs. "Same results both times. I know you're hoping there was a mistake, but the test was conclusive." She shoved her hands into her pockets, but not before he'd seen them shaking. "If you're not convinced, you're welcome to have it done again by another lab."

Staring at the graphs with their identical lines, he said, "I'll take your word that this lab knows what they're doing."

"I'm sorry. A positive paternity test is always a shock, even if you're expecting the result. It's even tougher when you're convinced it will be negative." Was she talking about him or herself?

"Don't feel sorry for me." He crumpled the paper in his hand. "I don't want your pity." Kat was the first woman since he'd been injured who had awakened anything at all in him. And now she felt sorry for him.

"If you don't want me to feel sorry for you, don't look so devastated at the thought of being Regan's father," she said hotly. "You have no idea what an amazing child she is."

He sat down heavily in one of the kitchen chairs. "It has nothing to do with Regan personally. I'm trying to figure out how this could have happened."

"How do you think? Didn't your father give you the birds-and-the-bees lecture?" she asked, her voice sharp.

His hand tightened on the paper, then he smoothed it on the table, flattening the creases where he'd crumpled it. "I know all about the birds and bees. And safe sex."

"I'm sorry," she said, jamming her fingers into her hair. Strands of bright red pulled free of her braid and curled against her neck. "That was a nasty thing to say, and I apologize. I know you're upset. I'm not real happy, either."

She hadn't been talking about his father, he reminded himself. It had been nothing more than a snide crack. Kat had a temper, and she had trouble controlling it.

When he found himself wanting to nudge her toward another outburst, he closed his eyes. Kat crackled with energy—the kind of energy he'd lacked in his life for a long time. She made him feel alive. She made him forget about his damn leg and his ruined career.

Which was pathetic and scary. He didn't need Kat, or anything about her.

He didn't want her, either.

"What's the next step?" he asked, trying to sound noncommittal.

She closed her eyes and he watched her trying to

steady herself. She bit her lip and smoothed her hands down her thighs. His own hands were clenched into fists, and he forced himself to relax. His heart slowed to a hard, steady beat as he waited for her to answer.

"That depends on you," she said, sliding into the chair opposite him. "The easiest thing, the most logical thing, is for you to sign the papers and let me finish adopting Regan."

"Easiest for who?" he asked. Certainly not him. He needed the cover of being Regan's father to continue his investigation.

"For Regan," she answered immediately. "She's just a little girl. She doesn't understand why her mother died and left her alone. How would she understand if you try to take her away from me?"

"What happens when she asks about her father? What do you tell her? 'He didn't want you? He signed some papers and walked out of your life?'"

"Of course not." She looked shocked. "I would never tell her that. I'd tell her we decided together that staying with me was the best thing for her." She hesitated. "Do you want to be part of her life? To visit her?"

Did he want to see Regan again?

See Kat again?

Yes. And the realization was alarming. "You have a pretty selective memory, don't you?" he said.

"What's that supposed to mean?"

"I told you last time we talked that I'm not going to sign any papers. Not until I'm satisfied."

"Satisfied about what? About whether I'm a suitable mother?" She smiled thinly. "A steady stream of social workers has come through my house in the last six months, checking on every aspect of my life. I'm sure they'd share their findings with you."

"I don't want to talk to any social workers. I'm not interested in platitudes or bureaucrat-speak. I like to figure things out for myself," he answered.

"You're going to judge me?" She gave him a scornful look. "Based on what? You've already said you don't have any experience with children."

"You don't have to have children to identify a good mother." He clenched his jaw. "Or a bad one."

She stared at him and he had the uncomfortable feeling that she was trying to see what was hidden inside him. He turned away. The only thing she would find in him was a vast emptiness.

"Are you going to contest the adoption?" Her low voice quivered with anger. Beneath it, he could hear her fear. "I know I can't stop you, but I'll do whatever it takes to keep Regan. She's my child now, and I'm not going to hand her over to you."

"She's my child, too." He nodded at the paper on the table. "According to those graphs, she has two parents."

"This isn't some fairy tale that ends in happily-ever-after," she said. He saw a flicker of fear in her eyes. "We're not going to end up playing house, being the mommy and the daddy for Regan." She hugged herself, as if trying to hold in her fear. "All that paper proves is that Regan has your DNA. That doesn't make you a father, Mr. Anderson."

He didn't want to frighten Kat. "We're both parents of the same child," he said, trying to smile. "I think, under the circumstances, you should call me Seth."

She flopped back in her chair. "You're trying to make a joke? The man who never smiles?"

Was that how she saw him? A grim, joyless man who kept his emotions under tight control? "First names are more friendly," he said.

"I'm not sure I want to be friendly with you, Seth." She emphasized his name.

"Not even for Regan's sake?"

He watched her struggle to control her temper. "If a snake comes into my house, I'm not interested in being its friend. I want it out of my house as fast as possible."

"Ouch," he said mildly. "You're comparing me to a snake?"

"You're a threat to me and to my family," she retorted. "And you'll be a threat until you sign the papers."

"I want what's best for Regan," he said. "I thought you did, too."

She shoved away from the table. "Of course I do. But it's not handing her over to a complete stranger who has no idea how to raise a child."

"And you do?"

"She's lived with me for six months," she said in a low voice. "Eight, if you count the time Holly was with me before she died. Of course I'm still learning how to be a parent. I'll be learning for the rest of her life. But at least she knows me. And I know her. I was her mother's friend. We have bonds that were forged over her entire life." She looked away. "All you have is a piece of paper with matching graphs."

"Then I guess she has to get to know me."

"What do you mean?"

"I mean I'm not going anywhere. I'm going to stay here until I'm satisfied that you're the best person to take care of Regan." He gave her a thin smile. "Or until I decide that you're not."

CHAPTER SIX

ANNIE SMITH WALKED out of the clinic into a gray dusk and locked the door behind her. "So long, Jenna," she said, and she watched until the girl had disappeared around the curve of the road on her bicycle. She double-checked the door before heading into the parking lot.

Kat was normally the last one out of the clinic, but today she'd left as soon as she'd seen their final patient. She'd been distracted all afternoon, and Annie was worried. In just a few days, Kat had gone from a conscientious doctor and considerate boss to a preoccupied, scattered woman. Something was wrong.

Barb thought so, too, but neither of them had any idea what was going on. Lost in thought, Annie fumbled in her purse for her car keys.

"Excuse me, Ms. Smith."

Annie jumped back, dropping her keys on the ground. Brady Morgan bent down to pick them up.

"Sorry to startle you." He handed her the keys.

Clutching her purse more tightly, Annie took the keys. "What's wrong?" she asked, suddenly frightened. "Did something happen to Hayley?"

"Hayley?" he asked, puzzled.

She drew in a ragged breath of relief. "My daughter."

The police officer shook his head. "Your daughter's fine, as far as I know. I didn't mean to scare you."

"Then what are you doing here? Are you investigating me? Is this about the ticket?"

"This isn't official business." His face went red and he glanced away from her. "I came to see how you were doing. If you're still upset about the speeding ticket."

"Ninety dollars is a lot of money," she said, grimacing. "Hayley's going to have to wait for her new soccer shoes. But I *was* speeding, so it was my own fault."

He tilted his head. "Why were you speeding?"

"Because I was late for work. I'd had a fight with my daughter and I was distracted." She shrugged. "And I drive too fast. Although I probably shouldn't admit that. You'll have everyone in the sheriff's department watching for me."

"Are you always this candid?"

"I'm not sure if the word is *candid* or *stupid*."

"It's refreshing, is what it is," Morgan answered. "I'm sorry I had to give you that ticket. But you didn't give me any choice."

"Don't sweat it," she said. "I deserved it."

"Since you're not mad at me, would you have dinner with me?"

Annie narrowed her eyes. "Are you asking me on a date, Officer Morgan?"

"It's Brady. And I am, yes."

"Why did you wait for me here? You had my home address from the ticket. Why didn't you call me?"

He smiled and Annie's heart kicked. "Some things are best done in person. Asking a woman you've ticketed on a date is one of them."

"You do that a lot? Date women you've met in the line of duty?"

"This is the first time," he answered. He shoved his hands into his pockets. "If you need a reference, talk to Kat. We went to high school together."

"Maybe I'll do that." When he'd handed her the speeding ticket, she'd felt a little zing. She hadn't realized he'd been interested in her, as well.

He scribbled on a piece of paper, then handed it to her. "When you make up your mind, give me a call."

"I'll do that."

He leaned closer, and his green eyes gleamed. "I'll look forward to hearing from you," he murmured.

He smelled like fresh air and pine, and she swayed toward him. Then he eased away and slid into his car, and she watched as he drove out of the lot.

She didn't need to talk to Kat. She already knew she wanted to go out with him, even though he was the cop who'd given her a speeding ticket. She smiled, bemused, as she watched Brady's car disappear. Life in Sturgeon Falls had suddenly gotten a lot more interesting. She was glad she'd listened to her ex-husband, Dylan, and moved here two months ago.

"HEY, KAT."

Charlotte Burns dropped onto the seat of the rowing machine next to Kat's and tossed a towel onto her lap. Kat eased the handle back into its bracket and slipped her feet out of the stirrups. Then she grabbed the towel and wiped the sweat off her face.

"What are you doing here?"

"Hello to you, too," Charlotte retorted.

Kat ran the towel over the back of her neck, then dropped it on the floor. "I'm sorry, Charlotte," she said. "I've been a little distracted."

"I figured that out when you didn't return any of my calls. What's going on?" Charlotte nodded at the monitor connected to the rowing machine. "Ten thousand meters? In thirty minutes? Are you trying out for the Olympics? Or are you just pissed off in a major way?"

Kat took a long drink from the bottle of water next to the machine. "How did you find me?" she asked.

"I called your office and talked to Annie," Charlotte answered. "She told me you'd come here. She also said you've been acting funny for a week of so."

"That's just weird," Kat muttered. "You're not supposed to be friends with your husband's ex-wife."

"Why shouldn't Annie and I be friends? I like her, and she and Dylan have been divorced for ten years." She grinned. "And joining forces is our only chance to survive Hayley as a teenager."

"Poor kid," Kat said, hoping to change the subject. It was usually easy to get Charlotte talking about Dylan and Hayley. "She doesn't stand a chance."

"That's the idea," Charlotte said with a laugh. She reached over and grabbed Kat's hand. "Now stop changing the subject and tell me what's wrong."

Kat picked up the towel from the floor and wiped sweat off the handles of the machine, then stood up and wiped off the seat. She and Charlotte had been friends since they were kids. They'd grown up together, Charlotte practically a member of Kat's family.

They *were* family now, since Charlotte had married Kat's newfound brother, Dylan. But Kat had no idea how to tell her about Seth.

Only because he was a threat to her. To the family she'd made with Regan.

It had nothing to do with the confusing feelings Seth stirred in her.

"Your parents are worried, too," Charlotte said quietly. "Give it up, Kat."

Kat threw the damp towel into one of the bins, finished her water, then tossed the empty bottle toward a garbage can, where it landed with a clatter.

Tossing the cap after it gave her a few more seconds to figure out what to say. Before she could speak, Charlotte towed her toward a pair of chairs in a corner of the room. "We all know something is wrong," Charlotte said. "Are you sick? Is Regan? Is something going on at the clinic?"

Kat shoved stray strands of hair out of her face and sighed. "I guess you'll find out sooner or later," she said. "Regan's father showed up."

"What?" Charlotte grabbed her hand. "He's here?"

"In the flesh."

"Did he sign the papers?"

"No." Kat extracted her hand from Charlotte's. "He says he has to make sure I'm a fit mother before he signs."

"What?" Charlotte jumped up and began pacing, slapping at one of the elliptical machines as she passed it. "You straightened him out, right? Did he back off when you clobbered him?"

"I didn't lose my temper." In spite of her worry, Kat smiled. She could always count on Charlotte to take her side. "He's right."

"What do you mean, he's right? We're talking about a guy who took more than five months to show up when he found out he had a daughter. And he's saying he's not sure you're a fit mother?"

"No. I mean he's right to check up on me. Regan is his daughter, even if he didn't know about her. He wants to make sure I'm the best person to take care of her."

"Why are you taking his side?" Charlotte stopped pacing and gave Kat a puzzled look. "What's going on?"

Kat wrapped her arms around her waist, trying to hold in the fear. "I'm trying to think about this logically. Objectively. Rationally. I've even thought about where I'd go if I have to run away with her."

"Oh, Kat." Charlotte dropped into the other chair. "Do you think it's going to get to that point? Would the court take her away from you and hand her over to a stranger?"

"Courts have done it before." The fear that was never far away twisted more tightly inside her. "He *is* her biological parent."

"No wonder you were rowing like you're possessed. What can I do?"

"Nothing." Kat reached for the woman who was as close as a sister to her, and hugged her tightly. "There's nothing anyone can do."

"I'll put Dylan to work. He has a lot of contacts from his days as an investigative reporter. Maybe he'll find something you can use in a custody hearing."

"Seth is a Secret Service agent. Dylan may be a good reporter, but I'm not sure how much he'd get from the government. They're pretty tight-lipped."

"If anyone can get information out of them, Dylan can." Charlotte grinned. "You still have a lot to learn about your brother. He's amazing."

"I may have only known him for a few months, but I figured that out right away." Kat touched the medal she wore beneath her T-shirt, the one that had helped Dylan find his family. "He showed up for every single one of Regan's soccer games this fall. Regan is crazy about Uncle Dylan."

"Believe me, the feeling is mutual. I know Dylan will do anything to make sure she stays with you."

"Thanks, Charlotte." Kat hugged her friend again. "It's only been a few days since we got the results of the paternity test, and I'm still trying to figure out what to do." She let Charlotte go and speared her hands through her hair. "Seth is a complicated guy."

Charlotte studied her intently, and Kat looked away. Charlotte had always been able to read her too easily.

"There's something you're not telling me," Charlotte said. "What is it?"

"Regan's father showed up and hasn't signed the adoption papers. Isn't that enough?" But she didn't meet Charlotte's eyes.

"There's something you don't want to tell me." She leaned to one side so she could look at Kat's face. "Oh, my God. You're interested in him, aren't you?"

"That would be really, really stupid," Kat answered, bending to fiddle with her shoelaces. "And I'm not stupid."

"You *are* interested in him! Kat, that's great! Is he interested in you, too?"

"How would I know? I don't know anything about him." She thought she'd seen a spark of interest the last time they'd talked. He probably thought it was as bad an idea as she did.

"Looks like you know enough." Charlotte bounced back in the chair. "When do I get to meet him?"

"I don't know. He'll probably want to meet the rest of my family. My 'support system.' But all I want is to have him sign the papers and disappear from our lives."

"You never could lie worth a damn," Charlotte said with a laugh. "This could be perfect."

"You're completely in love with Dylan and floating on a cloud of hormones right now. Clearly you're not thinking straight."

"I'm thinking straight for the first time in my life," Charlotte retorted. "And I know you better than anyone. Are you going to tell me you're not interested in this guy?"

"Okay, so I'm interested in him. That's just lust. Hormones. It doesn't mean anything."

"But it could. Give it a chance."

"I don't *want* it to mean anything. He could take Regan away from me. How can I think about getting involved with him?"

"You're already thinking about it."

Kat stared into the distance. "He seems like a lost soul," she said softly. "Like he's drifting through life. And there's something wrong with his leg. He limps when he thinks no one's watching, but he won't admit anything is wrong."

"Cross out thinking about it. You *are* emotionally involved with him."

"I told you—that would make me really stupid," Kat answered. "I need to stay as far away from him as possible."

"Don't close any doors, Kat. You never know what might happen."

"I don't know what I want to happen." She surged

out of her chair, restless and edgy. "And even though I want to stay away from him, I can't. I have to convince him to sign those papers."

"So see what happens. Get to know him. How tough is that? I'm not telling you to jump into bed with him. Just give him a chance."

"For God's sake, Charlotte! Who said anything about jumping into bed with him?"

Charlotte laughed. "I know what being a little interested leads to. I started out being a little interested in Dylan and look where I am now." Charlotte rubbed the ring on her left hand.

"Seth is not Dylan." Kat's voice was flat and she stood up. "And I'm not you. I adore you, Charlotte, but leave this alone. I can't handle you breathing down my neck about dating Seth. It's hard enough, trying to figure out how to handle this, without getting involved with Seth."

"I just want you to be happy," Charlotte said. Her eyes were full of love, and Kat felt as if she'd kicked a puppy.

"I know." Kat sighed. "I love you, CeeCee. I know you want me to be as happy as you are. This just isn't the right time."

"I'll call you tomorrow," Charlotte said. She hugged Kat again. "Don't worry. This is all going to work out. No one will take Regan away from you."

Kat wished she was as confident as her friend. She watched Charlotte leave, then cut through the weight room as she left. Time to get back to the office.

But as she walked past the equipment, she caught a glimpse of a dark haired man seated at a machine and her heart thumped against her chest.

It was Seth, wearing shorts and a faded T-shirt that said University of Wisconsin–Milwaukee. She opened her mouth to say hello, then she saw his leg.

His knee and thigh were crisscrossed with thick scars. Fresh ones. The muscles beneath them were smaller than those of his other leg, and Seth grunted in pain as he lifted weights with the injured leg.

She sucked in a quick breath, and Seth looked up.

CHAPTER SEVEN

"SETH," KAT MANAGED TO SAY. "I didn't expect to see you here." She glanced at his leg.

Seth picked up the towel on the floor, wiped his face, then dropped it casually onto his thigh. "I needed a place to work out and the guy at the motel recommended it."

Kat dropped onto the bench of the next machine. "What happened to your leg?"

"An accident." He shifted his leg, and she could see the effort it took for him not to grimace in pain. "What are you working on?"

"I come here to use the rowing machine." She nodded at his leg. "I've noticed you limping. Maybe I can help."

"You can't." His hands clenched the side of the bench. "The best surgeons in the military have messed with my leg for six months. There's nothing a GP can do."

"Ouch," she said, trying to sound casual. She'd

dealt with plenty of difficult patients, but she'd never taken their remarks personally. She shouldn't be taking Seth's personally, either. "I guess you told me."

He yanked the weight up again. "Sorry. I was rude. But some things can't be fixed, and I don't want to discuss my leg."

"It's your leg. Your pain." She shrugged. "I understand if you're scared to try something different. I'll talk to you later, Seth."

She was almost to the door when he said behind her, "I am not scared."

She turned around to find him scowling at her, his hands on his hips.

"Sure looks that way to me." She shifted her gym bag on her shoulder and smiled. "But you're right. Your leg, your business."

"I'm doing the exercises the doctors recommended. They're helping."

"Are you doing anything besides the exercises?"

"I don't believe in any of that woo-woo stuff."

"You mean alternative therapies that have been around for thousands of years?"

His mouth thinned. "That's exactly what I mean."

"Arnica is an herbal supplement that's used to heal bruising. Has anyone suggested that? Veterinarians use acupuncture on dogs, and it helps them. Which kind of blows the whole 'woo-woo' thing out of the water."

"So you think someone should stick needles in me and give me twigs and leaves to eat?"

"Arnica wouldn't hurt you, and it might help. Acupuncture, too. But I was thinking more of massage therapy."

"I've had massages. I've done nothing but rehab for the last five months."

Kat glanced at the cluster of scars above his knee. "You said some things can't be fixed, and I don't believe that. There's always more that can be done. You don't want to give it another try, that's up to you."

"You're saying that based on your experience in trauma medicine up here in North Podunk?"

She tightened her grip on her gym bag. Now wasn't the time to lose her temper. "I saw plenty of trauma during my internship and residency in Milwaukee."

"What does your *experience* recommend?"

Plenty of patients had tried sarcasm on her. It meant she was getting through to them. "There are a few things I'd try, but I'd start with the scars."

He draped the towel so it covered his leg, and she sighed. "I don't mean the external scars. There are scars beneath the skin." She lowered her voice when a young man walked in the door. "If you don't break them down first, you can sit at weight machines for the rest of your life and it won't do a thing for you. Regular massages can help with the scar tissue." She nodded toward the gym. "Andy, the physical therapist who works here, does a good job with massages," she said. "I refer a lot of my patients to him."

Without waiting for Seth to answer, she hurried out the door. When she got into her car, she saw him still standing at the door. Watching her. "You're a stubborn guy, Seth Anderson," she muttered as she accelerated away from the health club. "But you're not as stubborn as me."

KAT FINALLY RELAXED when the sounds of Kidz Bop drifted into the kitchen as she cooked spaghetti that evening. Regan sang along, off-key, and Kat watched her dance around the living room, the fake microphone in her hand. This was her life—coming home with Regan, eating dinner, doing homework. The mundane, homey details of being a family. Seth was no part of this world. In this house, it was just her and Regan.

As they ate dinner, Regan chattered about her day—what they did in school, who she played with at recess, the homework she had. Finally, she dropped her fork onto her plate.

"Shelby asked me to come to her house to play tomorrow. Can I?"

"You have soccer practice tomorrow. Maybe you

could play with Shelby this weekend. Do you want me to call her mom and see if she can come over here?"

"She can't." Regan spun the fork on her plate and didn't look at Kat. "She has to go to her dad's house this weekend. Her dad and her mom are divorced."

"That's too bad," Kat answered. "Maybe she can come over next week."

"Why do parents get divorced?" Regan stopped playing with her fork and looked at Kat.

"Lots of reasons, honey. Adult reasons." She paused, frantically wondering what to say. Surely other parents saw these minefields coming and had answers ready. "But it's never because of their children."

"Were my mom and dad divorced?"

Oh, God. How did she answer that? "No, sweetie. Your mom and dad were never married."

"How come?"

"They lived in different parts of the country," Kat said carefully, scrambling for an explanation. "Far away from each other."

"How come I never go to my dad's house like Shelby?"

"Do you want to visit your dad?"

"I don't know." Regan slid lower in her seat. "I don't want to go far away."

"Neither do I, sweetie." Kat prayed it wouldn't come to that.

"I want to stay here with you," Regan said in a small voice.

"And I want you here with me," Kat said, trying to sound cheerful. "Okay?"

Regan nodded, but she looked uncertain.

"How about we put the dishes in the sink and go read a book?" Kat said.

"Okay." Regan brightened. "Can we read Junie B. Jones?"

"You bet." Kat grabbed Regan and swung her into her arms, then carried the giggling girl into the living room.

THE NEXT MORNING, KAT WAS scribbling notes on one of her charts when Annie stuck her head into her office. "Patient in room one, Kat." She grinned. "Guess he just can't stay away from you."

"Who are you talking about?" Kat knew exactly who Annie was talking about, but she gave her nurse a quizzical look.

"Seth."

"You're on a first-name basis?" Kat raised her eyebrows to hide the jolt of disappointment. "Sounds like you're the one who's interested, Annie."

Her nurse shook her head. "It's not like that. He's just friendly. Barb and I were talking to him."

Friendly? Seth Anderson? "Whatever you say."

"I'm not interested in *him*. I'm going out with Brady Morgan tonight," Annie said, her eyes sparkling.

"Brady?" Kat wasn't happy about the rush of relief she felt. "Even after he gave you a ticket?" Kat asked.

Annie shrugged. "He apologized."

"Brady's a good guy," Kat said.

"He felt real bad about the ticket." Annie grinned. "I usually pay my own way on a first date, but I think I'll let him pick up the check this time."

"Sounds fair." She shrugged into her lab coat. "What is Mr. Anderson here for?"

"He didn't say. Just that he had some questions for you."

Kat took the thin folder that Annie handed her and walked into the exam room. "Good morning, Seth."

"I had a massage yesterday," he said abruptly. "It helped."

"Great." *Don't make too much of this,* she warned herself. He was probably at the end of his rope, ready to accept help from anyone who offered. It had nothing to do with her personally.

But she couldn't stop the little flutter of pleasure that he'd come to her. The brief moment of triumph that he'd listened to her. To hide it, she grabbed his chart and scribbled a note about his leg. "So what can I do for you today?"

His eyebrows rose. "You're not going to ask more questions? Probe a little more deeply?"

"You made it clear that whatever's going on with your leg is off-limits. I'm honoring your wishes."

He studied her for a moment, then smiled. It looked rusty from disuse. "Bull. You're teed off at me because I shot you down yesterday."

His smile made her feel giddy. And that sent off warning bells. "I hope I'm too professional for that." Her voice sounded disgustingly prim.

"You're not very good at hiding your emotions, Kat. I can see your temper in your eyes."

She tossed the chart onto the counter. Too hard. It slid across the surface and dropped to the floor.

Seth bent and picked it up. As he struggled to straighten, Kat saw his grimace of pain.

"Thank you," she said. Her temper disappeared, swallowed by concern. "Why are you here, Seth?"

Seth eased into the chair and extended his right leg in front of him, trying to ignore the throbbing pain. "You were right about the massage. It hurt like hell at the time, but my leg felt better last night. It sounded as if you had other ideas."

"I'm glad the massage helped. And I definitely have other ideas." She leaned back against the counter and smiled. A genuine one, and his gut tightened. "Do you want to tell me how you were injured?"

"Line of duty," he said, staring out the window. Remembering the pain of the injury, and the worse pain of the betrayal that had caused it. "Someone took a shot at the ambassador of a small central-European country."

"And hit you instead."

"That's how it's supposed to work."

"How long ago?" she asked, wrinkling her forehead. "I don't remember hearing about an assassination attempt on an ambassador."

"It was five months ago. And we kept it out of the papers." He massaged his leg. "Someone from the Service was involved."

"One of your own men shot you?" She straightened, an appalled look in her eyes.

"No." Banks had been too cowardly to take the shot himself. "He wasn't the shooter. But he told the guy where we'd be and when. And he let the guy into the perimeter."

"Did they catch him?"

"Oh, yeah." His smile was grim. "They caught the shooter and he gave up the guy who'd set it up. They're both in prison."

"Do you mind if I take a look at your leg?"

"Look all you want."

He stood up and unbuttoned his jeans, and she held up her hand. "Wait. I'll get you a gown."

"I don't need a gown."

Her eyes met his, and he couldn't look away. Awareness traveled between them, heating the air in the tiny room. *Wrong woman,* he told himself. But parts of him refused to listen.

"You sure?" She licked her lips, and his heart sped up. "I don't want you to feel exposed."

"Will it bother you if I'm exposed?" He slid his jeans down his hips.

"Not at all." Her mouth curled into a half grin and she glanced at his bare legs. It felt as if she'd touched him. "I'm a doctor. You have nothing I haven't seen before." Her gaze traveled up his leg and lingered on his boxers. "Except maybe those boxers. I wouldn't have figured you for silk, Seth."

"I'm full of surprises," he answered. More than she knew.

She sat down on the stool near the counter and picked up her pen. He felt a jolt of satisfaction when he saw her hand tremble. "Tell me about your injury."

The sensual haze abruptly dissipated. "I was shot in the lower thigh. Broke my femur, tore up a bunch of muscles. I got out of the hospital a couple of weeks ago."

"You were in the hospital for five months?" Compassion filled her eyes, soft and comforting. He wanted to drink it in. Instead he looked down at his leg.

"Surgeries and rehab."

"Is that why you never got the letter about Regan?"

"I guess so. Mail didn't seem real important. And when I got home, it took me a while to work through the pile."

"No one brought you your mail?" The compassion slid into pity, and he scowled.

"I didn't want it. Didn't want to be bothered."

She studied him, and he had the uncomfortable feeling that she knew. Knew there wasn't anyone who cared enough about him to bring him his mail. "Let me take a look at your leg," she finally said.

Her hand was warm when she touched his skin, smooth when she traced his scars. He shuddered. It had been a long time since a woman's touch on his leg had meant anything but more pain.

She froze. "Does that hurt?"

"No. It feels good."

Her hand stilled, lingered for a long moment, then dropped away. She drew in a breath. "You've had several surgeries," she said softly.

"Yeah, there were some complications." He wanted to feel her hand on his leg again. "Infections."

She checked his range of motion and gently palpated the muscles. Every time she touched him, sparks flew over his skin. Finally she moved away and shoved her hands into the pockets of her white coat. "You shouldn't be bearing all your weight on this leg yet. Why aren't you using a cane?"

"I'm sick of using a cane," he said. "I have to start walking sometime."

"You're pushing yourself too hard," she said. "But if you're determined to be an idiot, you can struggle for a while longer. Are you taking any painkillers?"

"Aspirin."

"I could give you something stronger."

"No, thanks. I was drugged to the gills for too long. No more."

"You can put your pants back on," she said, and she glanced at him again. At his shorts. He turned around and pulled his pants on, trying to hide the evidence of his interest in her.

"Got any ideas?" he asked, turning to face her again. He had plenty of ideas. None of them had anything to do with his leg.

"It took a lot of guts for you to come here today," she said. "I'm impressed."

"You were right about the massage." He shrugged. "I figured I might as well listen to your other ideas." And he'd wanted to see her again. That was both pathetic and scary. Especially since she was a suspect in a case.

"As I said before, I'd recommend the herbal supplement arnica. You can find it at health-food stores."

"I figured you'd say that. I already got some."

"Good." Shoving his file from one side of the counter to the other, she asked, "How are you sleeping at night?"

"I sleep." Not well, and it had been worse since he'd met her.

She nodded. "I'm going to give you a muscle relaxant. You can use it anytime, but it'll make you sleepy. I'd recommend using it at night."

"I don't need anything to make me sleep." No way would he take something that would make him groggy and dopey.

"Did I say I was giving you a sleep aid?" She pressed hard on the prescription pad. "Your muscles need to loosen up. You can take it any damn time you want, but you can't drive if you take it during the day."

"Fine. Give me the prescription." He didn't have to actually take the pills.

She scribbled on the next page of the prescription pad, then handed both sheets to him. "Here's a prescription for physical therapy. Have Andy massage that leg at least twice a week. Three times would be better."

"Thank you," he said, standing up. "I appreciate your advice."

"You're welcome."

He took a deep breath. "Will you and Regan have dinner with me tonight? To thank you for the help?"

"That's not necessary," she said. "Your insurance company will give me all the thanks I need."

A tiny smile tugged at the corners of his mouth. "Now I've pissed you off again."

She sighed and threw her pen on the counter. "Sorry. You seem to push all my buttons."

Lust speared through him. At least she felt something for him. Making her angry was better than leaving her indifferent. "Let me rephrase my question. Would you and Regan have dinner with me tonight? I'd like to spend time with you."

"It's not a good night to see how I am with Regan. She's always cranky after soccer practice."

"I didn't ask because I want to check you out. She's my daughter. You're the woman who's raising her. I'd like to get to know both of you."

"I guess it would be good for Regan to get to know you, too." She hesitated. "She asked me about her father last night. About why she never saw him. Do you want me to tell her that you're her father?"

"I don't know." Panic flashed through him. "I hadn't thought about it."

"I'm not trying to push you. But you *are* her father. If you want her to know that, I won't stop you."

"Not tonight," he said. What would he say to the girl? How would she act if she knew he was her father? How would she feel about him showing up now?

"Okay." She nodded, and he saw relief in her eyes. "Let me know if and when you want me to tell her."

"Thanks, Kat."

She gave him a shaky smile. "It's not easy, is it?"

"No." He ran his hand through his hair. "It would be easier to face a bullet."

Compassion filled her eyes again. "She's just a little girl, Seth. She's not going to judge you."

What would he say when she asked where he'd been for the first years of her life? "I'll keep that in mind."

She held his gaze and a whisper of awareness flew between them again. She turned away abruptly and shuffled through the papers in his file. "We can have dinner at my house—less pressure that way. Come over at six-thirty."

"Thanks. I'll see you then."

As he brushed past her and reached for the doorknob, she grinned. "Unless you want to give Annie and Barb the wrong idea, you might want to zip your pants before you open that door."

CHAPTER EIGHT

KAT FLIPPED THE PLASTIC BAG that held the marinating chicken and checked once more on the baked potatoes. The oven door slipped out of her hand and banged against the stove.

Get a grip. She'd been on plenty of dates. She couldn't believe she was this rattled about a man coming over for dinner.

Not just any man, she reminded herself. Regan's father. The man who would make the final decision about Regan's adoption.

A man she was attracted to, in spite of all the reasons it was a bad idea.

A really bad idea.

"I know how attraction works," she muttered as she slid plates on the table. "It's just his damn pheromones. I can ignore pheromones." No matter how strongly they enticed her.

The back door banged open. "I kicked the ball into the goal three times," Regan announced breathlessly as she bounded into the kitchen. "Once from far away. Just like I learned at practice."

"Good for you." Kat forced Seth out of her mind. "Let me see you do it again."

"Okay." Regan ran happily out the door and Kat followed her. The sun was setting, splashing the sky with orange and pink above the dark clouds hovering on the horizon. But there was still enough light to see the soccer net she'd set up for Regan at the back of the yard.

Regan dribbled the ball toward the net, then let go with a huge kick. It skimmed the side of the ball and sent it spinning off to one side. Regan stumbled and nearly fell.

"That's okay, honey. Try again," Kat called.

Determination on her face, Regan chased after the ball and unleashed another kick. This one trickled past the goal.

"That was a nice shot," Seth called from behind her.

Regan glanced at him over her shoulder, then kicked the ball again. "Was not. It missed."

"That's because you weren't kicking it right."

Kat turned around to see Seth leaning against the fence, hands in his pockets. "Hi," she said, self-conscious about the old jeans and sweatshirt she wore. She'd intended to change her clothes before Seth arrived.

He shifted his gaze from Regan to Kat. "I'm a little early. Sorry," he said.

"Don't worry about it." She gestured toward the gate. "Come on in the yard."

Regan ran over to Seth as he stepped through the gate, her too-large shirt flapping. To Kat's surprise, Seth was using a cane. He must have felt her watching him because he raised it a few inches and waggled it in her direction.

"What do you mean I wasn't kicking it right?" she demanded of Seth.

"Regan, say hello to Mr. Anderson," Kat said with a sigh. Sometimes her girl was frighteningly single-minded.

"Hello, Mr. Anderson. What did you mean?"

"You kicked it with your toe," Seth said. "You're supposed to use the side of your foot."

Regan looked skeptical. "How do you know?"

"I used to play soccer," Seth answered.

"Really?" Regan brightened. "Can you show me how?"

"Not tonight, Regan," Kat interrupted. "Mr. Anderson hurt his leg and can't run around the yard with you."

"That doesn't mean I can't show you how to kick a soccer ball," he said to Regan. "Go get that ball."

Regan raced to the ball and dribbled it back to

Seth. He had an odd smile on his face as he watched her. "You handle that ball pretty well, Regan."

"I practice a lot. I want to be as good as Hayley."

"Who's Hayley?" Seth asked.

"My cousin."

"Hayley is my brother's daughter," Kat explained.

"You have a cousin?" Seth raised an eyebrow at Kat. "And she hasn't shown you how to kick a soccer ball?"

"I mostly see her at night. When Kat is going out and Hayley babysits me."

Seth glanced at Kat. "When Kat has a date?"

"I don't know." Regan gave Kat a puzzled look. "What's a date?"

"It's not important," Kat said hurriedly. Her stomach jumped as she ignored Seth's sharp look. "If Mr. Anderson is going to show you how to kick a soccer ball, you'd better get busy. It's getting dark fast."

Seth balanced with his cane and used his injured leg to demonstrate the right way to kick a soccer ball. As Regan chased after the ball, he turned to Kat. "Sounds like you have a pretty active social life. I need to meet these guys," he said.

There were no guys. There hadn't been any guys since before Regan had come to live with her. But she wasn't about to admit that to Seth. "What I do in the evening is none of your business," she said.

"It is if it affects my daughter."

The slight emphasis on *my* daughter changed Kat's temper to fear. "It doesn't," she said, turning away to watch Regan. She was running toward them with the ball.

"Maybe I should decide that."

As Regan got closer, she said, "Nothing that I do when I go out in the evening touches Regan in any way."

"Then why won't you tell me about it?"

"I don't like being told what to do," she said.

Regan stopped in front of Seth before he could respond. "Did you see that?" she asked, flushed with excitement. "I made a good kick."

"You sure did," Seth answered. "Try it again."

As Regan ran around the yard, kicking the ball, Seth glanced at Kat. "I'm not letting this go," he warned.

"I'll consider myself warned." There was no real reason she couldn't tell him about the shelter, about what she did on those nights she went out. But he'd made her angry with his assumption that she had a string of men she was dating.

Trying to change the subject, she nodded at Regan. "Your suggestion seems to make a big difference."

He acknowledged her change of subject with a tiny smile, as if accepting it. For now. Then he looked back at Regan. "I can't believe she likes soccer," Seth said. He sounded almost wistful.

"Why is that hard to believe? A lot of kids play soccer, even in small towns like Sturgeon Falls."

"I loved it just as much as she does," he murmured.

Seth's bemused amazement touched her. Were all parents so astounded when they saw themselves in their children? She should be happy for Regan that her father had found a path to a connection with her, but her stomach churned with apprehension. "When you were Regan's age?" she asked lightly.

"I was older. High school. College."

"You played in college? You must have been pretty good."

He shrugged. "It was a way to get a college education."

"Your parents couldn't afford to send you to college?"

He tensed, then limped toward Regan without answering. "Try that kick with your other foot, Regan."

Kat watched them for another moment, then turned and walked blindly toward the house. Okay, so Regan and Seth were bonding over soccer. That didn't mean he was going to take Regan away from her.

It was a good thing, she tried to tell herself. Good for Regan.

Maybe even good for Seth.

Not for her. For her, it was every one of her nightmares come true.

REGAN CHATTERED TO SETH during dinner, telling him about her soccer team, her school and what they did at recess. Kat watched with a bittersweet ache in her heart. She'd prayed for Regan to come out of her shell, to be more like the animated, happy child she'd been before Holly's illness and death. She just wished she'd chosen another time to begin to emerge.

When Regan darted into the living room after dinner to decide on which books she wanted to read, Seth leaned back in his chair with a sigh. "She's pretty talkative."

"She hasn't been for a long time," Kat answered. "I guess *soccer* was the magic word." She picked up the dishes from the table and headed over to the sink.

"I liked talking to her." He sounded surprised.

"Regan is a great kid," Kat answered. "She's smart, she's funny and she's very sweet. It's torn me apart the past few months to see how sad she's been. I'm glad she's acting more like herself."

"It must have been hard for her to lose her mother."

Kat's hands stilled in the warm water. The depth of sadness, of loss in Seth's voice wasn't for a child he barely knew. Had he lost his mother at a young age? "It was horrible," she said, forcing herself to focus on Regan. "She was so lost, so quiet. So closed in on herself. Soccer and school have been really good for her."

"It sounds like you've been good for her, too," he said.

She twirled around. "I wasn't trying to spin something for you. To lobby for what I want. I was just…"

"Take it easy," he interrupted. "I'm trying to compliment you, Kat. That's all."

How could she take it easy? Seth held her life in his hands. If he refused to sign the adoption papers, if he contested Regan's adoption, she could lose Regan.

"I usually read to Regan after dinner," she said, drying her hands and not looking at him. "Do you want to read to her tonight?"

"You're being awfully generous," he said. "Letting me get to know her. Spend time with her."

"You're her father," Kat said quietly. "No matter what happens, that's not going to change. I would be hurting my child if I kept you away from her, and I'd never do anything that cruel." She used the towel to wipe down the stove. "Don't get me wrong. I want you to sign the papers. Regan belongs with me. But that doesn't change the facts."

"You're an unusual woman, Kat."

"I don't think so. I think most parents want to do the right thing for their children."

"I don't think everyone would feed their enemy grilled chicken and baked potatoes."

She faced him then. "Are you my enemy, Seth?"

"I don't want to be." His voice was low and hypnotic in the quiet kitchen.

"What do you want, Seth?" She didn't want Seth to be the enemy, either. What she wanted was far more complicated.

He took a step closer. "What I want might surprise you."

His eyes darkened, and Kat had no trouble reading them. Desire bloomed within her. "Maybe, maybe not. Tell me." She felt herself swaying closer to him. The rational part of her mind screamed at her to stop. The other part, the part that wanted darkness and heat and fire, soft murmurs and greedy hands, nudged her closer.

He touched her face, skimmed his hand down her cheek. Before he could do anything more, Regan appeared in the doorway. "I picked *Amelia Bedelia*," she announced.

Seth stepped away from Kat. "We were just coming into the other room."

No, we weren't. We were about to do something incredibly stupid. Kat tried to hang up the towel and dropped it on the floor. Tossing it onto the kitchen table, she followed Seth into the living room.

"I DON'T KNOW HOW YOU DO IT. I'm exhausted, and I didn't work all day today." Seth eased himself into an overstuffed chair in the living room after they'd put Regan to bed. The girl had insisted that both of them tuck her in, and he was surprised he'd enjoyed the ritual as much as he had. And the pink room with the white canopy bed had amazed him. How could someone who played soccer live in such a frilly room?

"Give yourself a break. You're still recovering," Kat said, sinking onto the couch. She was tired, too, if the bags beneath her eyes were any indication.

Maybe this was a good time to talk to her about her clinic. Her guard was down. She might let something slip that she wouldn't say if she was more alert.

"Do you work full-time at the clinic?" He ignored the shame that filled him. He was here to do a job. And that job involved talking to Kat about her office.

"Yes. It's my practice and I'm the only doctor."

"You own it?"

"Yes. Don't worry, I'm able to provide for Regan," she answered.

"Does everything have to be about Regan?" he asked.

"Right now, I think it does."

But her eyes sent a different message. He hadn't

been mistaken about those moments in the kitchen. He wasn't the only one interested. He told himself he could use that. "Do you really think so?" he murmured.

"Would you like a cup of coffee?" She bounced off the couch and nodded toward the kitchen.

"No, thanks. I'm having enough trouble sleeping."

"Then try the muscle relaxants before you go to bed. They'll help." She perched on the arm of the couch, as if poised to flee from a predator. She had good instincts, he thought grimly. He hoped she ignored them.

"Forget my leg," he said, watching her. "We've talked about my leg enough for one day."

"Fine. Then what would you like to talk about?"

"How about you? Tell me about your practice. How long have you owned it? How's it going? Tell me about the two women who work there."

"My practice is just as boring as your leg. Why do you want to talk about that?"

"It's called making conversation. Getting to know each other. I told you about my leg this afternoon. Now you can tell me about yourself." He tried to relax into the chair, to act as if it were a casual question.

She slid back onto the couch. "I've owned the practice for a year. It takes a while to get a business going, but we're doing okay. I can pay the mortgage and put dinner on the table every night."

"I like the two women who work for you. Barb and Annie, right?"

"Yes." She smiled. "They're good employees. Annie has only been working for me for a month or so, but she's a great addition."

"You're expanding your practice?" Maybe she needed money for that.

"No." She relaxed a little bit, apparently buying the getting-to-know-each-other line. "My previous nurse left—her husband was transferred—and that's when I hired Annie."

"It must have been tough, interviewing people while you're trying to see patients." He slouched in the chair, then noticed his foot was bouncing. Why the hell was he nervous? He interrogated people every day.

She smiled. It transformed her face and made his gut tighten. "Actually, hiring Annie was simple. She's my brother's ex-wife. He told me she was moving to the area, I was looking for a nurse, I talked to her and hired her. It was completely painless."

"You hired your former sister-in-law? That's pretty open-minded."

"I didn't know Annie when she was married to Dylan." She hesitated. "Dylan is my half brother, and I just met him a few months ago. My father didn't know he had a son until then."

"What was it like, finding out you had a brother?" he asked. As a child, he'd dreamed of finding a long-lost sibling. Being part of a family.

"It was strange at first," she said. "But Dylan is a great guy. And he married my friend Charlotte, so I got a package deal—a brother, a sister-in-law and a niece. And my parents were thrilled—they went from no grandchildren to two of them." She smiled. "Grandchildren they spoil shamelessly."

Her words hit Seth like a punch. He'd be taking Regan away from grandparents who loved her, too. It was a good reminder to stay away from the personal and keep his mind on his job.

"It sounds complicated," he said.

"No more than a lot of families." She smiled. "I got a great nurse out of the deal."

"Lucky for Annie."

"Lucky for me." Her mouth curved into a smile. "Although she's going on a date tonight and she's pretty excited. So maybe the move here was good for her, too."

"Yeah? Who's the lucky guy?"

"One of the sheriff's deputies. A guy I went to high school with. You met him the first night you were here."

"The guy who showed up when you called the police on me?"

Her smile dimmed. "That was Brady. And I'd do it again in a heartbeat if a guy I didn't know showed up and tried to get into my house."

"You did the right thing," he said. "And I hope it works out for him and Annie." Brady was a fast worker, he thought with satisfaction. He struggled to his feet. "I should let you get to bed. You probably have to work tomorrow."

"Short day," she said. "We're only open until noon on Saturday." She followed him to the door, and when he turned around abruptly, she was too close. But she didn't move away.

"Thank you for dinner," he said. He searched her eyes, and he saw longing there. He was afraid she'd see the same thing in his eyes. She took a step back at the same time he lifted his hand.

"You're welcome," she said, and he let his hand drop.

"Thank you for letting me spend time with Regan. You're right. She's a great kid."

"You can spend as much time with us as you like." Her voice was breathless and she cleared her throat. "With her."

He intended to. "I'll see you soon, Kat."

As he walked to his car, he felt her gaze on his

back. He wanted to turn around, to go back to her and explore what had flashed between them just now.

That would be a very bad idea. It would be dangerous in more ways than he could count.

CHAPTER NINE

"JENNA, YOU'RE SEVENTEEN WEEKS pregnant." Kat helped her shaken patient sit up on the exam table.

"No. I can't be," Jenna whispered. Tears dripped down her cheeks.

Kat took her sixteen-year-old employee's hand. "You said it's been four months since your last period," Kat said gently. "You've felt the baby moving already, haven't you?"

Jenna shook her head wildly. "No. That was just indigestion."

Kat laid the girl's clothes on her lap. "I'm going to wait outside the door while you get dressed. Then we can talk. All right, Jenna?"

The girl stared at her numbly, and Kat stepped into the hall. A few minutes later she knocked and walked back into the room. Jenna stood in her underwear, staring out the window, cradling her softly rounded belly.

"You're going to get chilled," Kat murmured. She

drew the sweater over the girl's head and guided her arms into the sleeves. Then she pulled on Jenna's baggy overalls.

"Have you told anyone else you thought you were pregnant?" Kat asked. Jenna stared at her, her mouth quivering, and Kat brushed the girl's hair out of her eyes. "Is Randy the baby's father?" Kat asked, holding her breath.

Jenna looked at the floor, flushing. "We used condoms," she said.

"Does he know you're pregnant?" she asked gently.

"I told him I thought I might be." She bit her lip. "He's the one who told me I had to talk to you."

"Good for him. I'm glad you came to me." So Randy was standing by Jenna. A lot of boys his age would have said they weren't the father and dumped the girl. In Kat's book, Randy got a lot of credit for stepping up to the plate. "What about your parents? Have you said anything to them?"

"No!" The girl spun around to face Kat, her eyes wide with panic. "You *can't* tell them. Please don't tell them."

"It's okay, Jenna." Kat took the girl's hand. "You're my patient and I can't tell your parents anything, even if I wanted to. Which I don't. All I care about right now is you."

The girl's mouth trembled as tears rolled slowly

down her face. "I don't know what to do," she whispered.

"Your parents are going to realize you're pregnant eventually," Kat said. She was surprised they hadn't noticed already. Jenna had been wearing overalls lately, and even though they were baggy, Kat could still see the swell of her belly. "Maybe you should tell them and let them help you."

"You don't understand, Dr. Macauley. If my parents found out I was pregnant, they would…" She shook her head. "I can't tell them."

"Do you have any aunts or uncles you can talk to?"

"No."

"How about your pastor at church?"

"That would be even worse," she whispered.

Kat shoved her fingers through her hair. This was the worst part of being a doctor—seeing her patients suffering and being helpless to ease their pain. On top of that, Jenna was an employee. A young woman she knew and cared about. "Jenna, are you afraid your parents will hurt you when they find out you're pregnant?"

The girl stared at her with too-old eyes. "I don't know what they'll do."

"Would you like to go to a shelter?"

"What difference would that make?" she asked. "I can't live in a shelter for the rest of my life."

"Of course not. But you could stay there until you figure out what to do."

"I don't want to have an abortion," Jenna said, biting her lip.

"You still have decisions to make," Kat said. "But you'd be safe at the shelter. The woman who runs it is a social worker, and she can help you sort things out."

"My parents wouldn't let me do that," Jenna whispered.

"You don't have to ask their permission to leave if you're afraid they'll hurt you, sweetheart. If you're not safe at home, you can't stay there." Kat glanced at her watch. "The clinic is closed. I could drive you to the shelter now, if you'd like."

Jenna's face turned white. "I have to go home. My parents will want to know why I'm late." She shrugged on her jacket and grabbed her purse from the floor. "Thank you, Dr. Macauley. Can you take the money I owe you out of my next paycheck?"

"Don't worry about it, Jenna." The girl wrenched the door open and ran down the hall. Kat waited until she heard the outer door slam before she stood up and walked to the front desk.

"Jenna seemed pretty upset," Annie said. "Is she all right?"

"I don't know," Kat murmured. "I hope so." She

tucked the girl's file under her elbow and headed to her office. "Go ahead and leave, Annie. I'll lock up."

She sat in her office, staring at Jenna's file, long after she heard the door shut behind Annie. She hated not being able to fix what was wrong.

Not being able to take away the pain.

She placed Jenna's file into her desk drawer and locked it. She didn't want Annie to see that file and find out Jenna was pregnant. Or Barb.

Kat pushed her fingers through her hair. How was Barb going to handle this news? Her receptionist was a capable, competent woman. She loved Randy. But Randy had been getting into a lot of trouble lately, and their relationship was strained. Kat stared at the locked drawer, wondering what she could do.

And Jenna. The girl wasn't just another patient. She worked for Kat. Kat knew her and liked her. There had to be more she could do.

She couldn't do a thing unless Jenna wanted her help. Frustrated, scared for Jenna, worried about Randy and Barb, Kat rubbed her forehead. She had to settle down. She was picking Regan up at her mother's, and she didn't want either her parents or Regan to see how worried and upset she was.

There had been too much worry, too much crying when Holly had first been diagnosed. Now, when Regan saw an adult upset, she was terrified.

As Kat stood staring out the window, trying to force Jenna out of her mind, she heard the door of the clinic open, then shut again. Had Jenna changed her mind about the shelter? Had she come back?

Kat rushed out of her tiny office, past her two exam rooms and down the hall into the waiting room. Seth was leaning over the counter, peering around the shelves of files.

"Seth. What are you doing here?"

"Hi, Kat." He smiled. "I was beginning to wonder if everyone had left and forgotten to lock the door. Where are Barb and Annie?"

It stung that he was looking for them and not her. And that was really childish. "They left a while ago," she said, pretending to straighten the information booklets on the counter. "I told Annie I'd lock up, but I've been busy."

Seth angled his head to see her face. When she tried to avoid his gaze, he took her wrist. "You're upset."

"I'm fine."

"What's wrong? Is this about Regan?"

"No." She extracted her hand from his grip. Reluctantly. "My last patient upset me, but I'm okay."

"Someone gave you a hard time?" Seth's face hardened. "I hope you threw him out."

"Nothing like that." If only it had been that simple, she thought as she headed for her office.

She got as far as the hall when he touched her shoulder. "Don't walk so fast. Unless you're trying to lose the gimp?"

She faced him with a wobbly smile. "You *do* have a sense of humor."

"Yeah, I'm a barrel of laughs." He tucked a strand of hair behind her ear. "What happened, Kat?"

She wanted to tell him. Wanted some reassurance that she'd done everything she could do.

She wanted to lean on someone else. Just for a moment.

"A teenage girl. Pregnant. Terrified to tell her parents." She swallowed hard, determined not to cry. "I know the baby's father and his family, but there was nothing I could do for her. Nothing. I had to watch her walk out of the clinic, knowing she was frightened, in trouble, and alone."

Seth smoothed away her frown with his thumbs. "You offered to help her, didn't you? Gave her some options?"

She wanted to press Seth's hands to her face and hold them there. "Yes. But she was too afraid. Too scared to go to the shelter."

"Maybe she needed time to think. She might be back."

"I hope so." She swallowed again, tasting the bitterness of failure. "I should have been able to do more for her."

"You offered. There was nothing more you could have done," he said. "You know that, Kat."

"There had to be something," she whispered.

He pulled her close, pressing her head against his chest. His heart beat steadily against her ear and his arms were strong around her. She felt as though he were holding her together. As if she'd fall apart when he let go.

"Do you bleed like this for all your patients?" he murmured, stroking her hair. "Do you cry for all the people you can't save?"

"She was so alone. She and her boyfriend have no one to help them make decisions. She has no one at home to hold her hand when she has morning sickness. No one to rub her back when she's scared."

"She's not completely alone." He stroked down her spine, fitting his body to hers. "She knows she can come to you."

She held on to him, savoring his warmth. The ease she found in his understanding.

Seth was the last man she should go to for reassurance. "Sorry," she said, letting her hands drop. "I don't normally fall apart like that. Especially on guys who are practically strangers."

"Are we really strangers, Kat?"

She touched a damp spot on his sweater. "I cried all over you." She forced herself to smile. "What was I thinking?"

"You think too much," he said, his voice deepening. "Sometimes we take comfort where we can."

He kissed her, his mouth soft and gentle as it settled on hers. She absorbed his taste, the glide of his lips against hers, the strength of his fingers as he gripped her more tightly. But as she kissed him, desire uncurled inside her. She wanted more than comfort from Seth.

She wrapped her arms around his neck and held on. Their bodies met from knee to chest, and she deepened their kiss.

Seth froze, then groaned deep in his throat. His hands roamed restlessly over her back. One tangled in her hair, anchoring her as he plundered her mouth. The other pressed her hip against him as if he was trying to fuse them together.

Desire flamed to life inside Kat, and she kissed him with an almost desperate need. When his tongue touched her lips, she opened her mouth and welcomed him inside.

His hand shook as he ripped open her lab coat. Her breast swelled as he touched her through her clothes, and she curled one leg around his, frantic to get closer.

He tore his mouth from hers and shoved up her

sweater, sliding his fingers against her bare skin. Her muscles jumped and her skin flamed where he touched her. When his mouth followed, she moaned his name.

He fumbled between her breasts to open her bra. The cool air caressing her breasts startled her, enough to cut through the fog of passion.

"Seth," she said against his mouth. "Wait."

"What?" he whispered, nibbling her lower lip. "What's wrong?" He cupped her breasts in his palms, brushing his thumbs across the tips.

The slow, rhythmic movement had her arching against him, shuddering with need. "What are you doing?"

He smiled against her mouth. "I'm kissing you. If you can't tell, I guess I have to work on my technique." His tongue caressed hers in time with his fingers on her breasts.

Her body throbbed with need. She wanted more, wanted to feel his skin against hers, his mouth on every part of her. But she called on all of her willpower and let him go.

"We have to stop," she said.

He stared down at her. "Why?"

"This isn't smart."

He bent to kiss her again. "The hell with smart."

She turned her head and his mouth touched her neck, making her shiver. "Seth. Stop."

He looked at their still-entwined fingers. "You don't look like you want to stop."

"I don't. But we have to."

He stared at her chest, and she realized that he could see her hard nipples through her sweater. She pulled her lab coat together and held it against her with a trembling hand. "This was a really bad idea."

He touched her cheek. "Didn't feel that way to me. Did it feel like a bad idea to you?"

"You know it didn't." She struggled with the snaps on the lab coat. Her bra still hung open and the brush of her sweater on her bare nipples was erotic and arousing. The lab coat secured, she wrapped her arms around herself. "For God's sake, Seth. We're not a couple of unattached people who can indulge a mutual attraction. Sex would only complicate the decisions we have to make."

"What's going on here has nothing to do with Regan. This is between you and me."

"That's not true and you know it." She shoved tendrils of hair off from her face, then pulled the band out of the end of her braid and finger-combed the curly mass. "You don't really know me. Maybe you'll assume that I jump into bed with anyone wearing pants. You wouldn't want your daughter raised by a woman like that."

"It was just a kiss. We didn't have wild sex on one

of your exam tables," he said with a smile. "Which sounds like fun, by the way."

It was a lot more than a kiss. But she could play it lightly, too. "The exam tables would be a bad idea. Too slippery."

Wrong thing to say. His pupils dilated and he reached for her, but she managed to elude him. "I'm not kidding, Seth. This was not smart."

His grin faded. "You're right. It wasn't. But it felt good. And it felt right. Not too many things have for the past several months. So I'm not going to apologize."

"I wasn't asking you to." She smoothed her lab coat. "But it can't happen again."

"Okay, we'll move on." He shoved his hands into his pockets and leaned against the wall. "I came here to ask if you and Regan wanted to spend some time with me this afternoon. It's a nice day to be outside."

"That sounds like fun," she said. The three of them needed to spend time together. And nothing could happen between her and Seth with Regan along. "Let me get my jacket and we can go."

It wasn't until she was driving to her parents' to pick up Regan that she realized he hadn't agreed that the kiss they shared couldn't happen again.

CHAPTER TEN

HE HAD ALMOST BEGGED.

It had taken one kiss. How could a woman reduce him to groveling with just one kiss? Especially a woman who was a suspect in a case.

He hadn't meant to kiss her. But she'd looked so desolate, so sad, that he'd had to hold her. He'd never been much of a comforter, but he'd wanted to calm Kat.

There was nothing calming about the kiss they'd shared.

Seth glanced over at Kat, who had both hands firmly on the steering wheel. She drove carefully, easing the small SUV around the curves in the road, edging out cautiously at the intersections of other small county roads. The lake shimmered behind the houses and through the trees on their right, deep blue in the sun. Behind them, Regan napped in her car seat.

What was Kat thinking? She wasn't an easy woman to read. Except when she'd been in his arms.

He'd had no trouble interpreting the little sounds she'd made when he'd touched her. Or the way she'd twined her leg around his.

Shifting on the seat, he watched the gulls dive into the water, then bob up to float on the waves, shaking water droplets off their feathers. The cold water looked good right now.

"Did you say something?" Kat asked, her voice pitched low.

Had he made a noise? "How long before we get to this park?"

"Another five minutes." She glanced over at him. "Is your leg bothering you, sitting this long?"

"It's fine." The last thing he wanted to talk about was his damned leg.

"Relax," she said. "I was just making sure you weren't sick. You haven't snapped at me all day."

"I've had other things on my mind." *Relax? Sitting this close to Kat? Wasn't going to happen.*

As she slowed for a stop sign, she glanced at him. His gaze locked with hers, and his heart began to race. Her smile faded as tension stretched between them in the suddenly too-small SUV.

A car roared around them, honking sharply, and it broke the silence between them. "I thought only cities had those kinds of drivers."

The SUV jumped forward as if Kat had pressed

the accelerator too hard. "We have our share. Tourists, mostly."

How long had they been sitting at the stop sign? Too damn long, if people had to honk.

"Why was that car honking?" Regan asked sleepily.

"Probably in a hurry," Kat said, her voice light. There was no hint of the need that had filled her eyes a moment earlier.

"Are we almost there?" Regan asked.

"Just about." Kat took a curve and a wide expanse of sand dunes stretched out to their left. "Cave Point Park is right after the dunes."

Five minutes later they pulled into a parking lot. There was a strip of grass and trees in front of them, then the blue of the lake. It looked as if they were on top of a small cliff.

Kat had barely parked when Regan began to fumble with the latch on her car seat. By the time Seth got out, she'd opened her car door, jumped out and run toward the cliff.

"Regan," Kat called sharply. "Stop. Wait for us."

Regan turned around and danced from foot to foot. "Hurry!"

Seth tried to walk faster, but Kat grabbed his arm. "Don't. The ground is uneven here. Be careful."

"I'm fine." He trapped her hand between his arm and his body, and he was surprised when she didn't pull away. He scowled. She probably thought he needed her to steady him on the uneven ground. But he didn't loosen his hold. He didn't care what she thought, as long as he felt her hand on him.

He heard waves crashing against rock before they arrived at the edge of the cliff. Kat let him go and grabbed Regan's hand, holding her tightly. Regan peered over the drop-off, her eyes alive with anticipation. "The waves are big today," she said.

"Grab her other hand, will you?" Kat asked him. "She's making me nervous."

Hold her hand? He'd never held a child's hand before. He reached out tentatively and she slipped her hand in his as if it were the most natural thing in the world. Her hand was so tiny. So fragile. She leaned over, and he instinctively tightened his hold. Their small chain stretched instead of breaking, the adults keeping Regan safe. Protected.

Water swirled wildly in and out of a small horseshoe-shaped formation in the rock in front of them, crashing against the stone. Every once in a while a plume of spray shot over the top of the rocks, covering them with a fine mist, and Regan squealed with delight every time.

To the left of the cave, the limestone bluffs ended with a long, flat platform of rock just above water level.

"Let's walk on the path along the top," Kat said.

"No!" Regan cried. "I want to climb down like we usually do. Please, Kat?" Regan tugged her hand out of Seth's and ran to the edge, and his hand felt empty.

He started to reach for her again but realized what he was doing and shoved his hand into his pocket. Kat glanced at him, and he saw in her face that she didn't think he would be able to climb down the ten-foot rock face. "What's down there, Regan?" he asked.

"Lots of good stuff," she said, jumping up and down. "You can walk along the rocks for a long way." She gestured to where the platform curved around another outcrop of rock and disappeared. "Sometimes I find seashells and sea glass down there."

"Then we should go check it out," Seth said. He lowered himself into a squat. "I'll go first to make sure it's safe."

"It's safe," Regan said, falling on her knees and looking down. "Me and Kat go down there all the time. Can I go first?"

"Does Kat let you go first?" Seth asked. When Regan didn't answer, he said, "That's what I thought." He eased himself over the edge.

Toeholds had been worn into the rock by countless sets of feet, but he had to balance on his good leg while he probed for one stable enough for his weak leg. His foot slipped off one and he winced, searching quickly for another.

Kat dropped to her knees above him. "Stop it," she said in a low voice. "We'll walk on the top today."

He ignored her and moved down another step. When he reached the bottom, he said, "Who's next?"

"Go ahead," Kat said to Regan. The child scrambled down like a mountain goat and immediately crouched to look in a tiny tide pool.

When Kat neared the bottom, Seth took her hand, helping her down the last step. Instead of letting him go, she drew him out of Regan's earshot.

"What's the matter with you? You could have hurt yourself, climbing down those rocks. We could have stayed on the top today."

"I wanted to climb down. I'm perfectly capable of figuring out what I can and can't do," he said. "I'm not six years old."

"Then why are you acting like you are?"

"Why are you acting like it's any of your business?"

"Because I don't want to see you splattered on the rocks when you slip and fall," she retorted. "Of course, you probably wouldn't do any damage to that hard head of yours. But I don't want Regan to see all the blood."

Beneath her tart words he saw real fear. Concern. No one had worried about him in a very long time.

"You're worried about me," he said, needing to touch her again but keeping his hands in his pockets instead. He glanced over his shoulder to check on Regan, but she was still crouched next to the tide pool.

"Of course I'm worried about you." She moved around him, heading for Regan. "I worry about all of my patients."

She had the last word, but he'd felt her hand shaking when she'd grabbed him. She'd been genuinely concerned about him. He was surprised how good that made him feel.

He joined Kat and Regan and asked, "What did you find?"

"A piece of green sea glass," Regan answered triumphantly, holding up a shard of glass that had been sanded smooth by Lake Michigan. She thrust it at Kat. "You hold it."

Regan stood up and ran closer to the water, and Kat scrambled to her feet. "Regan, get back. The waves are too rough."

"But that's where all the good stuff is," Regan protested.

"Can I take a look?" Seth asked.

"Sure." Regan scrutinized him. "But you might get wet."

"I like getting wet."

"Grown-ups don't like getting splashed," she said.

He almost smiled at the scorn in her voice. "I do."

"Okay." She took a step forward and slipped on the wet rocks. Seth caught her before she fell.

Holding the back of her jacket firmly, he said, "You're scaring Kat. You don't want to do that, do you?"

Regan shook her head. "No," she said in a small voice. "But I want to see if there's any sea glass out there. It's always close to the water."

"How about you stay with Kat and I'll look for the sea glass?"

She examined him doubtfully, he noticed with amusement. Being judged and found wanting by a six-year-old was a new experience. "You can tell me where to go."

He heard a muffled snort from Kat and glanced back to find her laughing. "Kat would love to be able to tell me where to go," he assured Regan.

"Okay."

Seth kept hold of her until Kat had taken her hand, then he lowered himself into a crouch. His leg screamed in protest, but he ignored it. Not disappointing Regan was much more important than the pain in his leg.

"Over there," Regan yelled, pointing to his left. "There's a piece."

He crab-walked to where Regan pointed and plucked a piece of brown glass from the swirling water. It looked like a remnant of a beer bottle.

He found two more pieces, another green one and a piece of blue glass that made Regan's eyes widen. "I never found a blue piece," she said reverently.

His leg was cramping and he struggled to stand. Kat grabbed his elbow and pulled him upright. "I can't believe you did that. It was really stupid," she murmured in his ear. "But thank you."

"It was my pleasure." And it was, he realized. Having Regan look at him as if he hung the stars had made his heart roll over.

Still holding his elbow, Kat steered him toward the path up the cliff. "It's time to go," she said. She held Regan with her other hand. "The two of you are soaked. It's too cold to play in the water."

He looked down at his jeans. They were wet from the knees down. His jacket felt wet, too. "I didn't notice."

"You have a lot in common with Regan," she said grimly. "She'd stay out here until she got hypothermia."

"Like father, like daughter," he said lightly.

Kat froze for a moment, then started walking again. She didn't look at him. "I didn't mean it that way."

"How did you mean it?"

"I was making conversation. Whining because the two of you aren't even cold and I'm freezing. That's all."

Kat had been very careful not to make any references to the relationship between him and Regan. She'd tried to keep it as impersonal as possible. "It's okay. I've had time to get used to the idea of having a child," he murmured.

Her hand tightened on his arm, then she let go. "I offered to tell her who you are," she said in a low voice. "You refused."

"Maybe I'm rethinking that decision."

She looked over at him, her eyes nervous. "Do you want me to tell her?"

He should say no. He had a job to do, a counterfeiter to catch. A counterfeiter who might be Kat.

After spending time around her, he doubted she was guilty. But he'd been fooled before.

Telling Regan he was her father would only complicate his job. But he wanted her to know. Wanted a connection with her.

He was a father. He looked at the child skipping along beside Kat and saw parts of himself. She didn't resemble him, but she had his passion for soccer. His determination. His stubbornness. "I'll let you know."

"All right."

They'd reached the path to the top, and Kat

scrambled up first, then helped Regan. When he struggled up the last foot, his leg on fire, she held out her hand to him. He hesitated only a moment before grasping it. He wasn't sure if he'd make it over the top without her help.

The wind swirled around him as they walked to her car, and he shivered. He'd been cold, inside and out, for the past six months.

Kat was quiet as they drove home, although she glanced at him occasionally. Each time, he felt as if she'd touched him. Regan chattered in the backseat, telling him about her sea glass collection. Acting as if she'd known him forever.

The circle that Kat and Regan made was a welcoming place. It was warm enough to drive away the chill. Did he want to be part of that circle, even temporarily?

He would be safer on the outside. He'd still be cold, but he'd be safe.

He glanced at Kat, then at Regan. Was it time to take risks again?

CHAPTER ELEVEN

MONDAYS WERE ALWAYS BUSY at the clinic. Thank goodness. Kat didn't want any spare moments to think. She'd done too much of that over the weekend.

After their outing to Cave Point Park on Saturday, they'd gotten pizza for dinner. Seth had talked to Regan and been a charming, friendly companion. Still, she couldn't stop believing he was anything but a threat to her. To her family.

Not even the memory of the kiss they'd shared could erase the fear. When she'd met him, he'd had no interest in being a father—or at least that was what he'd said. Now he was considering telling Regan he was her father. What was the next step? Was he going to contest the adoption?

And what if he did? He was Regan's father. He was a good man. How could she tell the court he didn't deserve to be a father to his child?

Chilled, she snatched a file from an exam-room

door. Forcing her personal problems out of her mind, she pasted a smile on her face and opened the door.

An hour later, she was in her office, getting ready to leave for lunch, when Barb stepped in. "Kat. I have to go."

Her receptionist's face was white and her hands were shaking. Kat jumped up. "Barb! What's wrong?"

"Randy." Her mouth began trembling and she looked away. "The high school called, and I have to pick him up. He was drinking in school."

"Drinking?" Kat stared at the other woman, shocked. "In school?"

"I have no idea where he got the liquor," Barb said. "Not at home, that's for damn sure. After his father left, I threw it all out."

"How did he get liquor into school?"

"In a water bottle." Barb gripped her purse more tightly. "Apparently, a lot of kids carry a bottle of water to class. Randy's was filled with vodka."

"I'm so sorry, Barb." Kat embraced the other woman, and Barb clung for a moment. "What can I do?"

"Not a thing, unless you can figure out what's going on with him." Barb stepped away. "Why he's been acting so wild lately. This is more than being upset about Craig. I don't know what to do." She huddled into her jacket. "He's been suspended for a week. I have no idea how to make sure he stays in the house during the day."

"Do you need to take time off?"

Barb grimaced. "I can't afford to."

And Kat couldn't afford to let her stay home with pay. "You can run home a couple of times during the day to make sure everything's okay," she said.

"Thanks," Barb said, her voice grim. "I'll take you up on that. And I'll get Craig to check on him, too. Randy just pulled his last stunt. He's grounded until he's thirty."

Kat watched Barb leave, her heart aching. She knew why Randy's acting out had escalated, but she couldn't tell Barb. She hoped to God Randy would.

She followed her receptionist up to the waiting room and locked the door behind her. "What's going on?" Annie asked.

"Barb didn't tell you?"

"I was in the restroom. I just saw her running out."

"It's Randy." She explained what had happened, and Annie shook her head.

"Poor Barb. It's so hard to be a single mother."

Annie had no idea how hard it had suddenly become for Barb. "You've been doing pretty well," Kat said, forcing herself to smile.

"Hayley's younger than Randy. And your brother is a great father." Annie's smile faded. "Not all kids are so lucky. Randy has a lot to deal with. No wonder he's angry all the time."

Scared was more like it. "I'm getting a real education in how hard it is to be a parent," Kat said.

Annie grinned. "This is the easy part," she teased. "When Regan is Randy's age, you'll be really nostalgic for the good old days."

If Kat still had Regan when she was sixteen. She turned abruptly and headed for her office. "I'll be back in a while," she said, grabbing her jacket and purse.

She needed to get away, to take some time to gather her composure, to plan. To figure out what she'd do if the worst happened—if Seth wouldn't let her adopt Regan.

She drove toward home too fast, only slowing down when she saw the sheriff's office in the distance. A speeding ticket was the last thing she needed. As she drove past the building, a car emerged from the parking lot.

It was Seth. She stared in her rearview mirror as his car turned onto the road behind her. What was he doing at the sheriff's office? Did it have something to do with her and Regan?

Or was it something else entirely?

A chill shivered through her. How well did she really know Seth?

RANDY MORRIS SLUMPED in the front seat of his mother's car, dizzy and sick to his stomach. Putting the vodka in his water bottle had been really dumb.

And he was stupid for getting busted. Now he was out of school for a week, and there was no way his mom would let him out of the house. How was he going to see Jenna? He sneaked a glance at his mom. She looked sad, and his stomach twisted again.

"How could you do this, Randy?"

He squirmed on the seat. He hated when she sounded disappointed. Why couldn't she just yell at him and get it over with? "I don't know."

"You don't know?" Her voice rose. "You just decided this morning to put vodka in your water bottle for no particular reason?"

"I guess."

"Where did you get it?" she asked.

"One of the guys."

"Which guy?"

Did she really think he was going to tell her? He gave her an incredulous look. He hadn't told the dean. He wasn't about to rat out Chet to his mom. "I don't remember."

"You don't remember or you're not going to tell me?"

He didn't answer.

She stopped at a red light and looked at him. He

squirmed again when he saw the pity in her face. "Your friend doesn't deserve your loyalty," she said in that quiet voice. "He isn't the one who got in trouble, is he?"

The light changed. "You know your father is an alcoholic."

"Yeah, yeah." He'd been glad when the old man had left. It was scary when he drank.

"That means even when you're an adult, you have to be careful about drinking." She swiped the back of her hand over her eyes. "You're scaring me," she whispered. "Drinking in school. During the day. And you're only sixteen. Why did you do it?"

He stared out the window, his eyes stinging. The vodka had seemed like a good idea this morning. Jenna had called him late last night, crying, and he'd had no idea what to do.

They pulled into the parking lot at the clinic, and he sat up. "What are we doing here?"

"I can't leave you at home alone until I search the house," his mom said. "I'm afraid you have more liquor hidden there. You're going to stay here the rest of the day."

She made it sound as if he were some kind of criminal, he thought, slamming the car door. At least Jenna would be working later this afternoon.

When they walked in the front door, Dr. Macauley

was talking to her nurse. Dr. Mac turned around. "Hi, Randy," she said, her gaze probing.

Feeling his face flame red, he mumbled, "Hi." He knew Jenna had told her about the baby, but he didn't think he'd had to face Dr. Mac so soon.

"I didn't want to leave him alone at home," his mom said. "Is it okay if he stays here until I leave?"

"Of course." Dr. Mac smiled. "There's an extra desk in my office, Randy. You can use it if you want to do your homework."

"Thanks," he said.

"He's not going to sit on his rear end all day," his mom said grimly. "I've got some work for him to do."

Three hours later, Randy dumped the bucket of dirty water into the sink in the utility room. He'd scrubbed all the baseboards in the clinic after cleaning the sinks and dusting every surface in the building. He'd seen Jenna come in, but he hadn't had a chance to talk to her.

Jenna stepped into the utility room. "Hi," she whispered.

He spun around. "Jenna." He pushed the door closed, then hugged her, feeling the hard bulge of her belly against his. "How are you feeling?"

"Okay. I haven't been sick to my stomach for a couple of days." She took a deep breath. "Dr. Macauley asked me just now if we've told our parents yet. I didn't know what to tell her, Randy. Every time I come into work, she asks me how I'm doing and how things are going at home. I'm scared she's going to tell them!"

"Dr. Mac wouldn't do that. She's cool." He stared at her, feeling helpless, not knowing what to do. He didn't want to tell his mom, either.

Jenna's mouth trembled. "I heard you got suspended," she said. "For drinking."

"Yeah." He rubbed his hands down the side of his jeans. "Stupid to get caught."

"That jerk Chet Howard gave it to you, didn't he?"

"Does it matter?"

"I need you to be at school," Jenna said. Her eyes filled with tears. She'd been crying a lot lately. "What am I going to do without you there?"

"You'll be okay," he said, panic tightening his chest. "It's only a week." He didn't want her to need him so much. Couldn't she suck it up for a week?

"I'm scared, Randy," she said, her voice catching. "What if someone at school finds out? What if they tell my parents?"

He glanced at her baggy overalls. They still hid her belly, but just barely. "No one's going to find out." He hoped. "I'll be back at school next week. We'll figure out what to do."

"Dr. Mac told me I need prenatal vitamins," she

said. "I don't have any money. My mom made me put my check in my savings account."

"I'll get some for you. Don't worry about the vitamins."

"Jenna?" his mom's voice called from the front of the office. Randy was ashamed that he was relieved.

"I'll call you tonight," she said as she slipped out the door. Randy nodded.

He rinsed the bucket once more, then tossed it on the floor. When it fell over, he kicked it before righting it. Everything in his life was totally rank. And he had no idea what to do about it.

CHAPTER TWELVE

KAT SHOVED HER HAIR OUT of her eyes and looked over the living room one more time. No toys on the floor, no books on the furniture. That was as good as it was going to get.

Seth would be here in fifteen minutes. They were going to tell Regan he was her father.

He'd called Kat at the clinic this afternoon and said he'd decided he wanted Regan to know who he was. When he'd asked if he could come over that evening, she'd forced the word *sure* out of her throat.

If Seth was going to sign the papers to let her adopt Regan, why did he want to tell her that he was her father? Just so he could disappear from her life? That made no sense.

Terrified that Seth wanted to take Regan away from her, Kat's first instinct had been to grab Regan and run. To disappear and start over somewhere far from Door County. The idea had been simmering in her brain since Seth had gathered sea glass for Regan.

No. The rational part of her brain took over. Seth didn't want to raise Regan by himself. He'd admitted that he had no room in his life for a child. No desire for one.

But the fear lingered, making her heart pound and her hands shake. *Things have changed since then,* the fear whispered. Seth had gotten to know Regan. Connected with her.

Facilitated by Kat herself.

Striding into the kitchen, Kat made a pitcher of grape Kool-Aid, Regan's favorite. Seth might be her father, but Kat *knew* Regan. Loved her.

Car tires crunched on the gravel driveway and she heard the slide of a minivan door opening. Regan burst into the house moments later, carrying her soccer ball. "Grape Kool-Aid!" she squealed, dropping the ball. "Can I have some?"

"Take your spikes off and put your ball away," Kat said. "Seth is coming over in a few minutes, then we'll all have a drink."

"Can I have some now, Kat? Please?" she begged, tugging off her shoes, then shoving them and the ball into the box in the laundry room.

"Okay." Kat poured a glass and watched Regan gulp it down. When she set the glass on the counter, she had a purple mustache.

"Go wash up," Kat said brightly. "I think Seth is bringing a pizza."

"Yay!" Regan grinned. "I love pizza."

"I know," Kat murmured as Regan dashed out of the kitchen.

When the doorbell rang, Kat took a deep breath and opened the door. Seth stood on the porch, leaning on his cane and holding two boxes from a chain pizza restaurant.

"Hi," she said, trying to smile. "Come on in."

He stepped into the house, watching her. "What's wrong?" he asked.

She shut the door a little harder than necessary. "What do you think?" she answered in a low voice. She looked over her shoulder to make sure Regan wasn't listening. "I have no idea how Regan is going to take this."

He stilled. "You don't want to tell her."

Of course she didn't. "I didn't say that. But this is going to be a shock."

"You can handle it any way you want. It's okay if you don't want to do it tonight."

She didn't want him to be so understanding. So respectful of her feelings. She didn't want him to be a man who was trying to do the right thing.

She wanted him to be a jerk. It would be so much easier to build a wall to keep him out.

"Let's eat before the pizzas get cold." She took the boxes and opened them on the counter. One was plain cheese, Regan's favorite.

The other was mushrooms and tomatoes. Her favorite. She gripped the cardboard box, unable to look at him. He'd been paying attention the last time they'd had pizza.

She wished he'd brought two sausage pizzas.

As they ate, Regan told him about school that day. Then, her eyes shining, she told him about soccer practice. "I told Coach Dave what you said about the kicks," she told him earnestly. "And I've been practicing them every day."

"That's great. But there's more to soccer than kicking the ball into the net, you know."

"Like what?" Regan gave him a doubtful look.

He leaned toward Regan, his eyes intent, and Kat clenched her hands together in her lap. *She* was the one who shared soccer with Regan. She watched her in the backyard, took her to practices and games, listened to her talk endlessly about the sport. They even watched soccer games together on television. All Seth had done was show Regan one lousy kick. Now he was the soccer go-to guy?

Stop it. She stood up and plopped another piece of pizza onto her plate. Being jealous of Seth's budding connection to Regan was small and petty.

"You have to be fast to be a good soccer player. Are you a good runner?"

Regan nodded vigorously. "I'm fast. Even Coach Dave says so."

"Is that right?" He smiled. "I was pretty fast myself."

Regan glanced at the cane he'd hung over the back of his chair. "Will you be fast again?"

Seth's smile disappeared and his eyes became carefully blank. "Faster than I am now, I hope."

"How about another piece of pizza, Seth?" Kat asked brightly.

"No thanks," he said without looking at her. "I'm good." He smiled at Regan, but it seemed forced. "I'd like to see how fast you are."

"I can show you now," she said, jumping up from the table.

"Hey, sweetie, you're not going to run very fast with all that pizza in your stomach," Kat said as she steered Regan to her seat. "Maybe you could show Seth how fast you are another time."

Seth glanced at her and she couldn't read his eyes. "How about tomorrow or the next day, Regan?" he said.

"I guess."

"It's a date," Kat said.

Regan looked from one of them to the other. "Are you and Seth dating?"

Kat caught her breath. "What do you know about dating?"

Regan shrugged one shoulder. "Ginny at school said her mom was dating. I asked her what that meant, and she said guys come over to their house and take her mom places." She looked from Kat to Seth. "She said her mom kissed the guys, too. Do you kiss Seth?"

"We're not dating, honey," Kat managed to say. "Seth is just a friend." And that was a big fat lie. She didn't want Seth for a friend. And he hadn't kissed her as if he wanted to be friends, either.

She felt Seth's eyes on her, and she finally glanced at him. She had no problem reading the question in his eyes. Taking a deep breath, she said, "Actually, Regan, Seth isn't just my friend."

"He isn't?" The girl looked bewildered.

"No," she said, smoothing Regan's hair away from her face. "He's here to meet you."

"He already met me." Regan furrowed her forehead.

Kat drew Regan into her lap. "I mean that's why he came to see us. To meet you." She watched Regan's face. "Seth is your father."

For a moment, Regan stared at her as if she didn't understand. Then she looked at Seth. "My father?"

"Yes, honey."

"My real father?"

"Yes."

Regan pressed against her, as if trying to get farther away from Seth. Kat clutched Regan's hand, and her small fingers trembled.

Seth watched Regan's eyes widen, then become guarded as she studied him. He waited for her reaction, his heart pounding. Who would have guessed Regan's response would be so important to him? That it would matter so much?

As Regan stared at him, she snuggled closer to Kat, who wrapped her arm around the child. It was instinctive, he realized. The seeking and giving of comfort and reassurance.

Two against one. No matter what fantasies he'd had on Saturday, he wasn't part of that.

"He can't be my father," she finally said.

"Why not?" Kat asked, her voice soft.

"Because my mom told me she didn't know where my daddy was. She didn't know how to find him."

"She didn't. We searched very hard for Seth, but it took a long time."

Regan watched him out of the corner of her eye. "How come he never looked for me?"

"Because I didn't know about you." Seth didn't wait for Kat to answer. "I came as soon as I found out."

Regan gave him a doubtful look. "If he's my father, how could he not know about me?"

Starting to sweat, Seth glanced at Kat helplessly. How was he supposed to answer that?

Kat pressed a kiss to Regan's hair. "He had to go away before you were born. That's why."

Regan swung her puzzled gaze back to him. "You were my father this whole time? Ever since we went to Mackeydoos?"

"Yes, Regan."

The girl scrunched her forehead. "Why didn't you tell me then?"

"It's complicated, Regan." He floundered, scrambling to explain. "I just didn't…"

"I didn't want him to tell you," Kat interrupted smoothly. She hugged Regan close. "I was afraid you'd like Seth more than you like me."

Regan looked astonished. "Why would I like him more?"

"He helped you with soccer. He found the sea glass for you."

"But you're my Kat," Regan said. "I love you."

"I love you, too, sweetheart." Kat rested her chin on Regan's head as she wrapped her arms around the girl. "More than anything. That's why I was afraid you'd like Seth more."

Kat was trying to make him look good. Why would she do that? This was her chance to turn Regan against him.

For Regan's sake, he realized with a jolt. She didn't want Regan to think badly of her father.

He stared at Kat, emotions roiling. Gratitude, pleasure, admiration of Kat's selflessness churned inside him. But guilt trumped all of them.

Kat was trying to smooth the way for him to get to know Regan. And he was using her, and her feelings for the girl, to investigate her clinic and her employees.

Never before had his job made him feel like slime. Never before had it twisted him into knots. But instead of getting up and leaving, he stayed put. This was the hand he'd chosen, so this was the hand he'd play.

"Do I have to live with you?" Regan's mouth trembled. "'Cause I don't want to. I want to be with Kat."

Kat tightened her arms around the girl until they almost looked like one being. A unit. Bound together by love and memories.

A family.

And he was the outsider, trying to tear them apart. "I just want to get to know you, Regan. Okay?" What was he supposed to say to this child? That he wouldn't take her away from her home? He couldn't promise her that.

He glanced at Kat, who was pale and shaken. She didn't look like a criminal. She looked like a woman sick with worry about her child.

She pressed another kiss to Regan's head and slid the child off her lap. "Why don't you go pick out some books? Seth and I will do the dishes, then we'll read. Okay?"

Regan looked at him doubtfully. "Him, too?"

"Sure." Kat smiled, but he could see the effort it took. "He has a name, sweetie."

Regan lifted her chin. "Seth."

Kat gave him a questioning look and he shook his head slightly. He wasn't going to insist that Regan call him *dad*.

The girl stood for a moment, as if waiting for a reaction, then finally turned and ran into the living room.

Kat took a deep breath and turned to him, her eyes fierce. "Now she knows. If you hurt her, I swear to God I'll cut out your heart."

"I don't have any intention of hurting her." But he might hurt "her Kat." He shoved away from the table.

"Sit still," Kat said. "You don't need to be on your feet. I'll clean this up."

"Stop worrying about my damn leg," he said, glancing toward the door so Regan wouldn't overhear him. "I'm sick of it."

Her hands stilled in the soapy water. "Sorry," she said stiffly. "I'm a doctor. I can't help noticing."

"I didn't mean to snap at you." He didn't want to fight with Kat.

He wanted to comfort her. To reassure her. To put his arm around her and tell her she had nothing to worry about.

It wouldn't be true. Three more phony bills had come through Kat's practice since he arrived, and he couldn't rule any of the women out. Brady hadn't uncovered any incriminating information about Annie Smith, although from the look in his eyes when he talked about her, he probably wasn't trying too hard. The background check on Barb Morris had revealed nothing but a failed marriage to an abusive drinker. Kat had a clean record, but it meant nothing. A sudden need for money could make the most honest person desperate enough to commit a crime.

Maybe she needed money for Regan's adoption. She'd never talked about how much it would cost, but it couldn't be cheap. Her finances had seemed straightforward, but maybe they needed to dig a little deeper.

He limped into the living room, where Regan stood at the door to her room, holding a stack of books to her chest. Her clear gaze made him squirm. He felt as if she could see inside him, know what he was thinking. Know that this was all a game. That he was using her as much as he was using Kat.

He shouldn't have told her. A moment of connection over soccer, a fun day at the park and all of a sudden he wanted to be a father. He shoved his hands into his pockets. What made him think he had any idea how to be a parent?

"We usually sit on the couch to read," Regan said, her voice challenging. As if she expected him to try and change their routine.

"I remember," he said. "Where do you want me to sit?"

She studied him for a moment, then she pointed to a spot on the couch. "There."

He lowered himself down and dropped the cane next to the couch. He planned on tossing it into the garbage. He didn't want Regan to ask him if he'd be able to play soccer again.

Kat walked into the room and smiled at Regan. "Let's see what books you picked."

She sat next to him and pulled Regan onto her lap. Her smile faded as she saw the first book in the pile. "We haven't read this in a long time," Kat murmured.

Regan pressed closer to Kat. "I want it tonight."

Seth leaned over to see the title. *Are You My Mother?*

He listened to the story about the little bird who'd fallen out of its nest who asked all the animals if they were its mother. By the time Kat was finished, his jaw was sore from clenching his teeth.

"What's next?" Kat asked, setting the book aside.

"I want to read that again." Regan snatched the book up again.

Kat glanced at him, then started reading again.

When she was finished, she stood up, still holding Regan. "Time for bed," she said cheerfully. "You have a big day tomorrow."

Seth sat on the couch, listening to the murmur of Kat and Regan's voices, the sound of running water, the rustling of sheets in Regan's room. What were Regan and Kat doing? When he was a child, he'd been told to go to bed, and that was it. No one tucked him in with soft words.

He wanted to leave, but it would be rude to walk out before Kat returned. He thumbed through a medical journal on the end table, spun the television remote control on the coffee table, crossed and uncrossed his leg. Finally the voices from Regan's room stopped and Kat emerged.

He grabbed his cane and pushed to his feet. "I'll see you later, Kat. I'll give you a call."

She blocked his way, her eyes blazing. "Not so fast. What's the matter with you?"

"What do you mean?" he asked cautiously.

"You told her you were her father, then hardly said another word to her all evening."

"I didn't know what to say."

"You had plenty to say when you were playing soccer with her. When you were at the park."

"She didn't know I was her father then."

"Now that she knows, you're struck dumb?" She crossed her arms and narrowed her eyes. "Besides telling her to call you Seth."

"What was I supposed to have her call me?"

"Why not 'Dad'?"

He looked away. "That's a name that has to be earned. I'm not her dad. I'm her sperm donor."

"You're her father. You could have acted like it."

"What was I supposed to do? Fake it? I have no idea how to be a father."

"And she has no idea how to have a father." The anger faded from her eyes. "You're making this too complicated, Seth. There aren't any rules for being a parent. Children don't come with instructions."

"Why did she read that book twice?"

Kat sighed. "We read that book every night for months after Holly died. Then it was a couple of times a week, then once in a while. She hasn't picked it at all since school started in September."

"This was a mistake. We shouldn't have told her I'm her father," he said, gripping his cane more tightly.

"You're scared," she said. She sounded surprised.

"Of course I'm scared." He didn't look at her. "I've never been anyone's father before."

"You were doing fine until tonight. Just relax and be yourself. She's not keeping score."

"I'm not so sure about that," he said, remembering the assessing looks she'd given him.

"This is hard for Regan, too," she reminded him. "She's gone through a lot in the last six months. Finding her father is going to take a while for her to absorb."

"You didn't have to throw yourself on the fire for me," he said. "You didn't have to tell her you were the one who delayed telling her."

"No child should think their father didn't want them," she said.

She was right. He knew from his own experience how painful that was. "It was generous of you to cover for me."

"I did it for Regan," she said.

Not for you. She didn't have to say the words. "I know it was for Regan. You're a good mother, Kat."

Hope sprang into her eyes, painful in its intensity. "Does that mean you're going to sign the papers? You're going to let me adopt her?"

"I don't know." He ran his hand through his hair. "I just found out I'm a father. I just told my daughter. I have no idea what I'm going to do."

"So you're going to leave me hanging? Going to make me sweat it out, a day at a time?"

"I'm not trying to torment you," he said. He reached out to touch her, but dropped his hand instead. "I have a lot to process here."

"Why did you have to come to Sturgeon Falls? You could have just signed the papers," she whispered. "It would have been less painful for everyone."

"Probably. But I'm glad I didn't," he said. "I wouldn't have met Regan. Now, whatever I decide, I know her." He touched her cheek, let his hand linger. "I never would have met you."

"This isn't about me," she answered.

He smiled. "No? It's not thinking about Regan that keeps me awake at night."

"Maybe it should be." She didn't move away from his hand, and he slid it down to her neck. Her skin was incredibly soft.

This is a mistake. On so many levels. But he couldn't look away from her. "I thought I was coming here because I had a child. I didn't know I'd meet someone like you."

"I'm the woman raising Regan. That's all," she said, but her voice was low and throaty.

He smoothed his thumb down her neck, and her pulse leaped beneath his touch. "You know that's not true. Regan wasn't around when I kissed you."

"You caught me in a weak moment."

"Is that right?" He lowered his head until his mouth hovered over hers. "I feel another weak moment coming on."

CHAPTER THIRTEEN

KAT STARED AT SETH, her heart pounding. His eyes had darkened until they were almost black, and his face was taut. She recognized desire when she saw it.

Especially when she was feeling the same thing. Heaven help her.

"Kat?"

Now was the time to back away. To use her head, to make the smart choice. But desire heated her skin and stirred her blood. It had been too late for the smart choice since the last time she'd kissed him. Since before that, if she was being honest. She stepped closer and touched his cheek.

Dimly she heard his cane clatter to the floor. Then he wrapped his arm around her. "I want you, Kat. I sure as hell didn't plan this, but there it is." He brushed his mouth over hers, nibbled her lower lip, and she sagged against him. "I can't stop thinking about you. About us. Together."

"Me, either," she said against his mouth. "Kiss me, Seth. Please."

As he kissed her, she tightened her hold on him. Maybe Charlotte had been right, she thought with a burst of hope. Maybe she and Seth should explore the attraction that raged between them. Maybe she should take a chance.

Maybe there was such a thing as a happy ending, after all.

Without taking his mouth away from hers, Seth walked her backward until her knees touched the couch. Then he swung her around, sat down and pulled her onto his lap.

The hard length of his erection pressed into her thigh, and he framed her head with his hands. As she moved restlessly against him, he burrowed beneath the T-shirt she wore. She felt the heat of each of his fingers through the thin lace of her bra as he covered one breast.

She moaned, and his hand tightened. Then he shoved the bra and T-shirt up and took her into his mouth. When he suckled her gently, she gasped and arched into him.

Her fingers scrabbled frantically against his shirt, trying to find the buttons. She needed to touch him, to feel his skin against hers. When she couldn't get the buttons open, she yanked the material out of the waistband of his slacks and slid her hand up his chest.

Like her skin, his was hot, and his muscles quivered wherever she touched him. She tugged impatiently at the barrier between them, and he lifted his head. "I want you naked, too," he breathed. "I want to look at you and touch you and taste you. For hours." He eased her off his lap and struggled to stand up, then he took her hand and led her toward her bedroom.

As they passed the door of Regan's room, the girl moved in bed, rustling the sheets. Desire disappeared in a cold rush, and Kat tugged on his hand.

"Seth, wait," she whispered. "We can't do this."

"Why not?"

"Regan is here." She nodded toward her room. "What if she heard us and woke up? What if she came to find me?"

He stared into the room for a long time, watching his daughter sleep. He sighed. "You're right." He drew her away from the door and leaned in to kiss her. "I'm sorry. I didn't think. Worrying about kids is a new one for me."

"For me, too," she said.

He smiled. "So when you go out at night and leave Regan with her cousin, you're not going on hot dates?"

"Only in my dreams." She walked back to the living room and picked up his cane. "It's probably just as well," she said. "We need to think while we're rational and decide if we want to take this further."

"I don't have to think about it," he said. "I know I do."

She glanced down at his slacks, which were still tented. "I can see that. I meant think about it with your big head."

He grinned. "I like you, Kat Macauley. Can I take you out on a date? Just you and me?"

"I'd like that," she said. "How about Saturday night?"

"You're going to make me wait five days? How about tomorrow?"

"Regan's school is having a program tomorrow night. The Harvest Moon," she said, rolling her eyes. "The schools are too PC to have Halloween programs anymore."

"What's a harvest moon program?"

"Singing, mostly. That's what the other moms told me. Each grade performs a few songs." She leaned against the door. "Would you like to come?"

"Will Regan be singing?"

"Yes, of course. She's been practicing her songs for weeks."

"I'd like that."

After agreeing on a time to meet, Seth opened the door. "I'll see you tomorrow," he said. He kissed her again, and she wanted to clutch him closer.

As he straightened, he touched her face. "I'll make

a decision about Regan soon, Kat. But whatever I decide, I don't want to lose touch with her. Or you."

He limped down the steps, the light flashing off his cane. It had started to rain, and water glistened in his hair. She waited until he'd gotten into his car, then she closed the door.

She turned around to find Regan standing in the hall. "You were kissing Seth," she said.

"I was, yes." She scrambled for an explanation. "I was saying goodbye to him."

Regan studied her. "He didn't kiss me goodbye."

"Did you want him to?"

"I don't know." She scrunched her face as if she was going to cry.

"It's okay, Regan." Kat swooped the girl into her arms. "I know it's a lot to figure out. We'll figure it out together, okay?"

Regan nodded, the top of her head bumping Kat's chin. Kat held her close as she carried Regan into the darkened bedroom.

RAINDROPS PLAYED A HOLLOW melody on the thin roof of the rental car as Seth stared at the house. The living-room light beckoned, and he could see Kat's red hair over the curtain that covered the bottom of the window. He wanted to walk to the door, to go back into the house. To kiss her again, to feel her kissing him. But before he moved, his phone chirped at him. When he glanced at the screen, he saw he had a message.

"Call me." Brian Carlson's voice was brusque, and Seth sighed. He'd forgotten about protocol, about checking in regularly.

He punched in the number. "Anderson here," he said when Carlson answered the phone. "You've been trying to get hold of me."

"Hell, yes. What's going on? Why haven't you been giving me updates?"

"I've been too busy trying to solve this case," Seth retorted.

"A phony hundred showed up at a new store yesterday. I left you a message and expected you to call me back. I thought you had a lead on this case."

"I said I had a connection. And I'm working it."

"Work it faster," Carlson said. "I'm getting pressure from Anstley to clear some of these cases."

He'd lost his stomach for this job, and he didn't give a damn about Carlson's boss or the Service bureaucracy. He wasn't in the mood to pretend otherwise. "Yeah," Seth said and closed the phone.

Kat had disappeared from view while he'd talked to Carlson, and that was just as well. For a moment he hadn't been thinking. He'd been imagining he could have a real relationship with Kat. That there could be something between them besides lies and deception.

He started the car with a twist of the key. Kat was a suspect. That made her off-limits.

She was also the mother of his daughter. The bond between Kat and Regan was deep and strong.

And he might be the man who had to sever it.

THE MURMUR OF VOICES FILLED the school gym as Kat walked in with Seth. The stage at one end of the gym was decorated with construction-paper pumpkins, moons and colored leaves. Several rows of risers stood in the center of the stage.

"Hey, Kat," Becky Torres called, and Kat smiled at her mother's friend. Jerry Kramer, one of her dad's fishing buddies hugged her, and a high-school classmate grinned and waved. Everyone looked at Seth, then back at her, questions in their eyes.

This had been a mistake. She should never have brought Seth. Not only was everybody speculating about Seth and their relationship, but Regan had been totally silent on the drive to the school.

She and Seth sidestepped four people and slipped into two vacant seats. Kat busied herself by taking off her coat and arranging it over the back of the metal chair. It had been so long since she'd been out with a man in Sturgeon Falls that she'd forgotten about this aspect of small-town life. By tomorrow, everyone she knew would have heard about her "date."

She barely noticed the kindergartners performing as she tried to figure out when she could visit her parents to tell them about Seth. As she mentally scanned her schedule, the youngest children were filing off the stage. Then the first graders walked on.

The children filled up the risers. Regan was in the front row, and she stood rigid, plaiting her skirt. They'd picked the red dress out together, and Kat had curled Regan's hair for the performance. Red barrettes in the shape of butterflies held the curls away from her face.

"Do you see her?" Kat whispered to Seth.

"Yeah. She's cute."

"Be sure to tell her," Kat answered. "She's very proud of that dress."

The music teacher nodded to the pianist and the first chords of "Pumpkin, Pumpkin on the Ground" rolled through the room. The children started singing, but Regan didn't open her mouth. Instead, she stared at the audience.

Kat gripped the seat of the chair. Regan was terrified. What was wrong?

As Regan looked around the gym, she backed slowly away from the other children. She got tangled in the curtain on the side of the stage until it completely enfolded her. Finally, her teacher appeared and unwound her from the curtain. When she tried to urge Regan back to her place with the other children, the girl shook her head violently. Kat could see she was crying.

She grabbed her coat and edged past the people sitting next to her. She heard Seth behind her, but didn't wait for him as she hurried out of the gym and around to the side door to the stage. Regan's teacher had her arm around the sobbing child, and she shrugged when she saw Kat. "I have no idea what happened."

Kat scooped Regan up. "What's wrong, baby?" she whispered.

Regan wound her arms around Kat's neck and clung to Kat's waist with her legs. "I want to go home," she sobbed.

"Okay." She stroked Regan's curls away from the girl's damp face. "Let's get your coat."

She set Regan down at the door to her classroom and the girl ran in and shrugged on her coat. Kat said to Seth, "I think she was just overwhelmed by everything. She's been so excited about this program."

"And I ruined it for her."

"Don't blame yourself." This was *her* fault. She should have realized it was too much for Regan to handle. "Kids have meltdowns all the time."

"It would have been fine if I wasn't here."

Kat didn't say anything.

The ride home was silent except for Regan's

sniffles. Kat kept glancing in the rearview mirror, but Regan was looking out the window. Finally Seth shifted in the passenger seat to face Regan. "Your dress is pretty, Regan," he said.

"It's new," she said without looking at him.

"Those things in your hair. Are those butterflies?" Seth asked.

Regan fingered the barrettes. "I like butterflies," she said softly.

"Yeah? I do, too," Seth said. "I had a butterfly collection when I was a kid."

Regan stole a glance at Seth. "Real butterflies?"

"Yep. I had fourteen of them."

"Where did you get them?"

"I caught them."

Kat grabbed Seth's arm. "No killing," she mouthed. Regan still checked for worms on the sidewalk when it rained. She'd be horrified to think about killing butterflies.

"How did you catch them?" Regan asked.

Seth glanced at Kat, worried. Then he turned to Regan again. "I had a net."

"What did you do after you caught them?" she asked.

Kat's hand tensed, and he squeezed it. He'd figured out what she meant. "I let them go," he said. "I just wanted to look at them."

Regan studied him. "How could you have a collection if you let them go?"

His kid was too smart. "Sometimes I found dead ones," he said, searching for an answer. "Those were the ones I saved."

"I never saw a dead butterfly."

"You have to look very hard." Seth shifted in his seat, trying to ignore his throbbing leg. He didn't like lying to Regan. "Have you ever been to a butterfly conservatory?" he asked her, trying to steer the conversation away from dead butterflies.

"What's that?"

"It's a big building that has all kinds of butterflies flying around. You can walk through it and see them up close. Sometimes they even land on you." There was a spark of interest in Regan's eyes. "Would you like to go to one sometime?" he asked.

Regan looked at Kat, driving the car. "Kat, too?" He barely heard her voice.

"Of course. Kat, too."

Regan settled back in her booster seat, eyeing him thoughtfully. "Maybe."

THE NEXT DAY, KAT WAS PAYING bills in her office when Annie stuck her head in the door. "Your dad is here, Kat. He wants to talk to you."

Kat tossed her pen onto the desk. "Send him in."

Gus walked in. "Hi, Dad," she said, giving him a hug. "How are you feeling?"

"Nothing wrong with me," he said, hugging her back. He eased off until he could see her face. "What the hell's going on with Regan?"

"You heard about what happened at the school program last night," she sighed.

"Did you think I wouldn't? Jerry Kramer told me first thing this morning." He scowled. "He told me you brought a date, too."

Kat sank into her chair. She should have known Gus would find out about Seth. The grapevine in Sturgeon Falls was frighteningly efficient. "He wasn't a date, Dad. That was Regan's father."

"Her father?" Gus stared, then sat down heavily. "He finally showed up?"

"He's been here for almost two weeks."

"What the hell did he come here for? And why is it taking so damn long for him to sign the papers?"

"The DNA test took five days. And he hasn't decided yet if he's going to sign the papers."

Gus's eyes narrowed. "We gonna meet this guy?"

"Please, Dad," Kat said quietly. "I have to handle this. Okay? It's complicated."

Gus studied her for a moment, then he stood up. "Regan needs to go fishing," he said. "Take her mind off her troubles. We'll all go on Saturday. Hayley's been bugging me to go out once more before the end of the season, anyway."

"I can't take her fishing on Saturday. I have to work."

"Dylan, Charlotte and I will take her." He grabbed her hand. "Kid needs to be with her family. We'll get on the lake and spend some time with her."

"Thanks, Dad." Fishing was Gus's cure for everything. "I think that's just what Regan needs." She walked down the hall with him. "Give Mom a kiss for me."

She stopped dead as she stepped into the waiting room. Seth leaned against the counter, talking to Annie, but when he saw Kat, he straightened and smiled. "Hi," he said.

Kat looked at her father and sighed. "Dad, this is Seth Anderson. Seth, my father, Gus Macauley."

"It's a pleasure, Mr. Macauley," Seth said, holding out his hand.

Gus shook it, then jerked his chin at Seth. "This him?"

"Yes."

Gus nodded. "We'll be keeping an eye on you, Anderson," he said, then he clomped out the door.

"What was that all about?" Annie asked, wide-eyed.

"You know how my father is," Kat answered. "Mr. Protective."

Annie looked from her to Seth. "Yeah, I heard about the mystery man at the school program last night," she said with a grin.

"Of course you did," Kat muttered. "I'm sure there's no one in Sturgeon Falls who hasn't."

Seth looked from one of them to the other, an intrigued look on his face. Kat turned and headed for the hall. "Come on back to the office, Seth."

She closed the door behind them. "At least half of my patients have quizzed me about my 'date' last night," she said. "And as you saw, my father came by. I told him you were Regan's father."

"I figured. No wonder he went cave-man on me."

"Cave-man?" In spite of herself, she laughed.

Seth shrugged. "He was protecting you and Regan. I'm guessing it's automatic with fathers and daughters."

Kat's smiled disappeared. "What are you doing here, Seth? I know you're not here to discuss the latest Sturgeon Falls gossip."

"I have a proposition for you."

Heat curled inside her. "Yeah?"

He smiled, but his eyes darkened. "Not that kind of proposition. That's a standing offer. This is business."

"Really? What kind of business?"

"I'd like to go to work for you, Kat."

CHAPTER FOURTEEN

"WORK FOR ME?" SHE STARED at him. "Doing what?"

"Why don't we talk about this at lunch?" he said, reluctant to talk where Barb and Annie could overhear them. He liked both the women, but they were still on his list of suspects.

Kat hesitated, then shrugged. "I have to eat, I guess."

He didn't say anything more about his proposal as they were seated at the Cherry Blossom Diner and placed their order. Over the surrounding noise of silverware on plates and the murmurs of conversation, she asked, "What did you mean about working for me? I don't need protection."

"I wasn't talking about protection. You need help organizing your office. Specifically, how you handle money."

"I do not!"

"Yeah, Kat, you do." He stretched his leg out beneath the table and accidentally bumped hers. He didn't move, and neither did she. "You're pretty haphazard. Barb and Annie just toss your money into that metal box. They don't keep track of who paid or how they did it."

"They write it on the patient's record."

"You should keep a separate log every day of who paid and how much."

"Why is this your business, anyway?" she said, moving her leg away from his.

He shrugged, as if he didn't care what she did. "It's not. But I thought I could be helpful." He unwound the napkin from the utensils and made a production of putting it in his lap. He'd been prepared for Kat to resist his suggestion. She was a very self-sufficient woman.

The waitress slid a bowl of mushroom soup and a BLT in front of Kat, and a hamburger in front of him. Kat took a bite of her sandwich as she studied him. Finally she said, "This isn't a cash business. Most of our patients have insurance, so any cash we get is co-pays. Frankly, I don't worry about the cash because we never have more than a couple hundred dollars at the end of the day."

"Yeah, I get that, but you should still be keeping track of it. Didn't your accountant set up a system for you?"

She took another bite of her sandwich. "It was too complicated. Barb complained about it, and I couldn't figure out how to fix it. So we ignored it."

"I can fix it for you."

Kat's spoon clanked against the soup bowl as she narrowed her eyes at him. "Maybe I like it just the way it is. What's this really about, Seth? Is this about taking care of Regan? Do you want to know how much I make? I'll show you my books."

"It's not about Regan." He reached for her hand, holding it tightly when she tried to pull it away. "It's about me. I'm going nuts without any work to do. I can only rehab so many hours a day, and I think I've seen every inch of Door County." He forced himself to smile, to hide the sick guilt that flowed through him. "Yesterday, I was desperate enough to visit the Spike O'Dell Coffee Cup Museum."

Her eyes softened as he spoke, and he felt even worse. "I love that place," she said with a smile. "Did you see the cups signed by Dan Quayle and Henry Kissinger? I think they're right next to the Hugh Grant and Frankie Avalon ones."

"It's quirky, that's for sure." The din of the diner made him lean closer. "I need to keep busy," he said. "I think I can help you. That's all this is about."

She tugged her hand away. "So you just woke up this morning and decided you wanted to work for me?"

"Not exactly," he lied. He'd spent the night figuring out how to get more access to Kat's practice. "I came by to see how Regan was doing."

Kat slumped against the booth and pushed the remains of her sandwich around on her plate. "She was a little quiet this morning."

"Did she tell you what happened?"

"I'm not sure she knows herself." Kat arranged her silverware and didn't quite meet his eyes. "I think it was what I told you last night. She was overwhelmed and had a meltdown."

"It was because I was there," he said flatly.

"That was probably part of it, although she never said so." She shoved the plate away. "Think about it, Seth. First we tell her you're her father, then the next night she's performing for the first time in front of a crowd. A crowd that included her father. No wonder she couldn't deal with it."

He was shocked how much her words hurt. "Should I stay away from her?"

"Of course not. She needs time to get used to you. To get used to the idea of having a father. Regan is as nervous and uncertain about your relationship as you are."

That was impossible. He was here to find out if Kat was a counterfeiter. To find out if he had to take Regan away from Kat. Her mother.

Regan couldn't possibly be more worried than he was.

"Like I said, I was concerned about her." At least

that was true. "That's why I stopped by. You were in an exam room, and Barb and Annie were trying to figure out how much money should be in the cash box. I was struck with inspiration." It had only taken a few careful questions to start their discussion.

She scowled. "They shouldn't be talking about office business in front of you."

"I think they've figured out I'm not just a patient."

"I haven't said a thing to them about you," she said.

"They have eyes," he said dryly. "They can put two and two together."

To his surprise, she turned pink. "I didn't think it was that obvious."

He was afraid *he* had been. For the first time in his career, he hadn't been able to focus completely on the job.

After a restless night, he'd realized he had to find out, one way or another, if Kat was involved with the job. His feelings for Kat and Regan were getting too complicated, but before he could untangle them, he had to deal with the counterfeiting.

He had to do that as fast as possible. Because when he was with Kat, he wasn't thinking at all.

Trying to hide his desperation, he shrugged. "It's up to you. I don't want to step on any toes. But since I have so much free time and nothing to do, I thought I'd offer."

Kat studied him thoughtfully. "So by letting you fix what's wrong with my bookkeeping, I'd be doing you a big favor. Is that what you're saying?"

"In a nutshell." Guilt nudged him again. She could be signing her own arrest warrant.

She shrugged. "It's not how I would spend my free time, but if you want to spend your days working on my accounting problems, go ahead."

"Thanks." He glanced at the bill and put money on top of it. "You saved my sanity."

AFTER THEY RETURNED to the clinic, he spent the afternoon talking to Barb and Annie between patients and watching how they collected the cash and checks. They both had plenty of opportunities to manipulate the money in the cash box. Kat, on the other hand, hadn't once gone near the cash.

When the office closed, Kat stuffed the money in the bank deposit bag, then shoved that in her purse. "You don't count the money here?" he asked.

"I do it at home," she said with a questioning look. "Why?"

"Just trying to get a feel for how you do things. Do you always deposit the money?"

"Mostly. Barb's done it once or twice, when I've needed to pick Regan up early."

So he couldn't rule out any of them.

As they were leaving the office, the phone rang and Kat picked it up. "Here she is," she said after a moment. She handed the phone to Barb and waved Annie out the door.

As the receptionist listened, her face went white. "I'll be right there," she finally said, dropping the phone in its cradle.

"What's wrong?" Kat asked, her eyes scared.

"It's Randy," she whispered. "He was caught shoplifting." She stifled a sob. "Brady is at the store with him. I'm going to meet them there."

"What can I do?" Kat asked.

"I don't know." Barb looked at her, tears pooling in her eyes. "I don't know what to do with him."

"Why don't I go with you, Barb?" Seth offered. "Maybe I can help."

"How?" Barb asked, biting her lip. "You can't keep him out of jail."

"You shouldn't go alone," he said, taking her arm and leading her out of the office. He glanced at Kat. "Go get Regan. I'll come over later."

She nodded, looking at Barb, and Seth realized she knew something. About Randy?

He watched as Kat got in her car, then he put his hand under Barb's elbow. "Why don't I drive?"

When they arrived at the drugstore, they found Randy sitting in the storage room at the back of the store, surrounded by shelves filled with cardboard boxes. Staring at the floor, wearing loose jeans and a Green Bay Packers sweatshirt, he looked very young. Brady Morgan stood next to Randy, along with a thin, dark haired man wearing khakis and a blue dress shirt. He wore a tag that said Manager and swallowed when they walked in, his Adam's apple bobbing nervously.

"Randy," Barb cried. "What did you do?"

The boy shrugged without looking up.

"Randy Morris, look at me," she demanded.

When he raised his head, his eyes were red. "What?"

"What's going on, Randy?" Barb whispered. "Why are you doing all these things? What's wrong?"

His eyes filled and he looked away. "What did he take?" Barb asked the manager.

The young man shook his head. "A couple of bottles of prenatal vitamins," he said. "Dumb-ass kids. They think it's funny to steal something goofy." He glanced at Randy. "Last week a boy tried to steal tampons."

"Prenatal vitamins? Randy, what…"

Seth put his hand on Barb's arm. "I'm Seth Anderson," he said to the manager. "I'm a friend of Barb's. Are you going to press charges?"

"That's our store policy," the manager said. "That's why I called the cops."

Barb bit back a sob. "Oh, my God." She grabbed the cop's arm. "Brady, are you going to arrest him?"

"Afraid so, Barb." Morgan sounded apologetic. He glanced at Randy. "Shoplifting is a crime."

Randy scrunched lower in the chair, and fear filled Barb's eyes. "What are we going to do, Seth?"

Randy glared at him. "Who are you?" Beneath the defiance, Seth saw fear and humiliation.

"I'm a friend of your mother."

Randy sneered at Barb. "You couldn't come by yourself?"

"You should be grateful for all the help you can get, Randy," Morgan said. Morgan's eyes were full of sympathy as he gazed at Barb. "I'm sorry, Barb."

Seth needed to take control of the situation. Barb was falling apart and Randy wasn't helping his cause with his attitude. "How much are the vitamins?" Seth asked the manager.

"Twelve bucks a bottle."

"You owe him twenty-five dollars," Seth said to Randy. "Okay, Morgan, cuff him and take him in."

Barb gasped, and Seth squeezed her arm. "We'll meet you at the sheriff's office," he said to Brady.

After Randy had been walked through the store and out to the patrol car, Seth turned to the manager. "I understand if you have to press charges. We apologize for the trouble he caused."

The manager sighed. "I've known Randy for a long time," he said. "He was on my brother's baseball team last summer. He's a good kid."

Barb started to speak but Seth interrupted. "Good kids do stupid things all the time. Sometimes the only way they learn is by dealing with the consequences."

The manager nodded toward the front of the store. "I think Randy will be dealing with the consequences for a while. Those girls near the cash registers are in his class. Everyone at the high school will know he's been busted for shoplifting." He looked at Seth and Barb. "I'm not going to press charges," he said. "Maybe this will scare him into straightening up."

"Thank you," Barb choked out. "Thank you so much."

The manager crossed his arms. "I would have pressed charges if you had asked me to give him a break. You did the right thing." He glanced from Seth to Barb, obviously assuming they were a couple. "I think he's going to be in enough trouble at home."

"He certainly is," Barb said grimly.

"The trip to the police station in handcuffs should make a big impression, too," Seth said.

After they were in the car, Barb asked, "Why did you tell Brady to go ahead and arrest Randy? I would have begged Brady to let him go."

"That's why I butted in. I figured we'd have a

better chance if we didn't try to buy or bully our way out of it. Police officers don't like it when parents try to clean up their kids' messes." He drove away from the drugstore. "A few hours in a cell isn't going to hurt Randy. Maybe he'll think twice next time he's tempted to do something stupid."

"You want me to leave him in jail?" Barb asked. She sounded horrified.

"Yep. I want you to go home and have dinner. Take your time. Maybe watch a television show or two."

"Brady's going to wonder where I am."

"No, he won't. I'll go over and explain."

Barb bit her lip as she stared out the window. "Thank you, Seth," she said, her voice wobbly. "For going with me and handling it for me. You didn't have to help me, and I appreciate it." She glanced at him. "You knew just what to do. You must have kids of your own."

Seth stared out the window, seeing the stars twinkle in the midnight-blue sky. So Kat hadn't told Barb who he was. He wondered why. "I have a daughter," he finally said.

"She's a lucky girl," Barb said quietly.

KAT PACED THE LIVING ROOM, watching for headlights on the road. Regan was already in bed and Kat hadn't heard from Seth.

Barb must be frantic. And poor Randy. First drinking in school, and now shoplifting. Classic acting out. Her heart ached for him and Jenna. It would be terrifying to be sixteen and dealing with a pregnancy alone.

Gravel crunched on her driveway and she hurried to the window. Seth was walking slowly toward the house. She threw open the door and waited for him to walk inside.

"Is he okay?" she asked.

"He's fine," he said as he eased down to the couch. "He should be getting home about now."

"What did he take?"

"Prenatal vitamins," Seth said, watching her.

Kat drew in a quick breath, and Seth's eyes sharpened. "What on earth did he do that for?" she said, trying to cover her slip.

Seth pinned her with his eyes. "You know what this is about, don't you? Why does Randy need prenatal vitamins? Did he get someone pregnant?"

"I can't talk to you about this."

"But you know what's going on." It wasn't a question.

She curled into the chair across from him but couldn't look at him. "Yes, I do," she said quietly.

"Why haven't you told Barb? She's beside herself with worry."

"I know, and I feel horrible. But I can't tell her. Patient confidentiality."

"That's mean," he said. "Letting Barb suffer like that."

"I'd tell her if I could. But I can't." Kat jumped up from the chair and stood at the window, staring out at the night sky. If she could only wish on a star and solve Randy and Jenna's problems. Or at least confide in Seth and ask for his advice. She was shocked at how strong the urge was to do just that.

"Is this about more than a pregnancy? Does it involve something illegal?" he asked. His voice became more urgent, and she turned to look at him.

"Of course not. If it was illegal, I wouldn't keep it a secret." She managed a smile. "Is that the first reaction of people in your line of work?"

"Yeah, I guess it is. I always expect the worst."

Her smile faded. "That's no way to live."

"I'm realistic. I see things for what they are. And I'm never disappointed."

"That's awful."

"Better than being a Pollyanna."

"You don't think I'm realistic? After four years of medical school and another three as a resident in an inner-city hospital?" She glanced away. "Believe me, I see things exactly as they are. But I choose to hope for the best."

"In my line of work, hoping for the best can get you killed." He rubbed his leg.

"Maybe you're in the wrong line of work."

He shrugged. "I like my job. Or at least I did before …"

"Before you were shot?" she asked quietly.

"Yeah." He struggled to his feet. "Before my leg was wrecked. Before I couldn't *do* my job."

"Your leg will heal."

"Not enough," he said, his voice bitter.

"Not enough for what?"

"To get back where I was when I was shot. On the protection detail."

"You don't know that."

"Yeah, Kat. I do. I just don't want to admit it."

Her heart ached for him. "Give it some time," she whispered, taking his hands. "Keep doing your rehab. You might be surprised."

"There's that Pollyanna streak of yours again," he said. He smiled, but it didn't reach his eyes.

"Everyone needs hope, Seth."

"I'll stick with reality." He limped toward the door. "I'll see you at the office tomorrow."

CHAPTER FIFTEEN

ON FRIDAY, SETH TOTALED the figures on the pad of ledger paper, his fingers flying over the adding machine. Barb and Annie had gladly given him complete responsibility for the money, telling him he was welcome to the job. They had enough to do, they claimed, dealing with the patients and the insurance forms.

No counterfeit bills had turned up since he'd started working in the office. Was it just coincidence? Or did the guilty person suspect why he was there?

Kat was the only one who knew he was a Secret Service agent. The knowledge hung over his head like a dark cloud, drifting into his consciousness whenever he let down his guard. Kat couldn't possibly be a counterfeiter, he tried to tell himself. He *knew* her. Knew her integrity went bone-deep.

Just as he'd known the agent who had betrayed the team, he reminded himself grimly. That error had cost him a functioning leg and six months of his life.

"You about done with that money?" Kat called from her office. "We need to get going."

"Just about," he answered, pulling the wad of cash out of the metal box.

He flipped through the fives and the tens, counting quickly, turning each bill the same way. There were two twenties, then a hundred-dollar bill. He froze.

No patient had given them a hundred-dollar bill today. He'd been there the whole time the office was open and had made every entry on the log.

He didn't have to touch the bill to know it was a fake.

Since the amount of cash tallied with the log, someone in the office had put the bill in the box and removed an equal amount of smaller bills.

Kat, Barb or Annie. They were the only ones who'd been here today.

"Are you thinking about running away to Mexico with all that cash?" Kat leaned against the doorway, smiling. "You'd get as far as Iowa, I bet."

He shuffled the counterfeit in with the rest of the bills. "This piddling amount of money? Nah. I'm waiting for a really big day to take off."

"You can finish that at home," she said, shrugging into her coat. "Regan's waiting."

Home. He liked the sound of that. Too much. He stuffed the money and the log sheet into the bank bag and grabbed his own coat. "Let's go."

A half hour later, he followed Kat and Regan into the house. The already familiar scent of their home, a mingling of Kat's spicy citrus and Regan's little-girl sweetness, drifted over him. He'd spent every evening that week with them. Kat wanted him to spend time with Regan. And he wanted to spend time with both of them.

Today, as Kat hung up their coats, he handed Regan a paper bag. "I got something for you today."

Regan looked at the bag, then up at him. Cautious excitement filled her eyes. "You did?"

"Go ahead and open it," he said.

Regan eased the bag open and took out a book and a folded piece of paper. "It's about butterflies," she said, staring at the cover, her eyes lighting up. "That's a monarch." She paged through the book, a beginner's guide to butterflies. "Are all these butter-flies around here?"

"No, but some of them are." Seth sat down on the couch. "Do you want me to show you how to tell?"

She hesitated for a moment, then she nodded and slid onto the couch next to him. "Yes, please."

Out of the corner of his eye, he watched Kat pick up the piece of paper that had fallen to the ground. As she read it, her face softened. Finally she handed it to him. "Thank you," she said.

Seth tucked the paper into the back of the book as he showed Regan how to use the maps in the guide.

A FEW HOURS LATER, KAT STUDIED Seth over the rim of her wineglass. Regan was in bed and the house was quiet. "Regan really liked that butterfly book," she said.

"I hope so." He'd treasure the memory of the excitement in her eyes as she'd looked through it. And the fact she'd chosen it for her bedtime reading. It was the first time this week she hadn't asked for *Are You My Mother?* "I enjoyed sharing it with her."

"Why didn't you tell her what that piece of paper was? That it was for a butterfly kit?" Kat asked.

"I didn't know if you wanted to tell her now or wait until later. The butterfly chrysalises won't come until spring."

"Will she be here when they arrive?"

"I don't know, Kat." He'd made a mistake. Subconsciously, he'd been planning for the future. A future with Kat? With Regan? With both of them?

The phony hundred-dollar bill sat in the deposit bag in Kat's purse, but he could feel its malignant presence from across the room. He took a drink of wine, but it tasted sour.

Kat set her glass of wine on the table, and the red liquid sloshed over the rim. "What do you mean, you don't know? You're jerking me around, Seth."

"And you're trying to back me into a corner. I can't tell you what I don't know." He gulped the wine, felt it burn down his throat.

"When will you know?"

"When I do. Okay?"

She watched him for a long moment. "This is hard for me," she said quietly.

"I know. I'm doing the best I can." Maybe the phony bill would hold some clues. "Can we change the subject?"

"Fine," she finally said. "Tell me about the butterflies. Why did you start collecting them?"

"They were beautiful. And I loved watching them fly."

"Fly away?" she murmured. He pretended he didn't hear her.

She shifted on the couch. "Where did you grow up?"

"A small town west of Milwaukee. I doubt you've heard of it."

"Try me," she answered lightly.

"It doesn't matter," he said, staring out the window. The darkness was complete—he saw nothing but his reflection. "I've put that part of my life behind me."

"How come?"

His fingers tightened around his wineglass, then

he set it down. "I prefer to live in the present. I've told you about my job and what I do."

"But not about where you came from." She crossed her arms.

"Because it's not important. What you see is what you get."

"You know that's not true. You can't run away from the past."

"Yes, you can. I have. And I want to leave it in the past, where it belongs." He reached for her, needing to touch her. To make her see that *this* was what mattered, the connection they'd forged between them. Not the past. "This is who I am, Kat. Not some kid growing up in a hick town who didn't know…" He pulled her close. "Who didn't know he would meet someone as incredible as you."

He bent to kiss her, but she slid away from him. "I know you're a private person, and I'm trying to respect that. But I feel as if I'm only getting to know a shadow. That the real person is hiding behind it."

Kat was too perceptive. He *was* hiding from her. And until he found out who was passing counterfeit money through her practice, he couldn't step out from the shadows.

"I won't be hiding in the shadows tomorrow night," he said. "I can't believe we have a whole evening together. Alone."

"Maybe we can get to know one another," she retorted. "Just because Regan is going to stay with my brother and Charlotte and Hayley doesn't mean we're going to do anything but talk."

"Talk is good." His eyes darkened. "But I can think of better ways to get to know each other."

Her eyes heated, but she said, "What's going on between us is more than sex, and I think you know it." She watched him steadily, and he wanted to squirm. "I don't *know* you. And I don't sleep with men I don't know."

"Maybe we can fix that tomorrow night," he said, picking up his jacket.

"I hope so." She smiled, but he saw the sadness in her eyes.

THE NEXT MORNING, SETH BACKED through the door of the clinic, carrying coffee for Barb, Annie, Kat and Jenna. Two patients were already sitting in the waiting room. "It looks like it's going to be busy today," he said.

"We're booked up," Barb said. "And Jenna isn't here yet."

"She and Randy must have had a hot date last night," Annie teased.

"Nope. Randy is grounded until he's ready for Social Security," Barb said grimly. "The only time he's been out of the house was when he brought me my checkbook yesterday."

Seth froze as he wrote the headings onto the new cash log. "Randy was here yesterday?" he asked, keeping his voice light. "Has he turned into an invisible man?"

Barb smiled. "He came in over lunch. I'd forgotten my checkbook and needed it to go shopping after work."

"So he was your delivery boy."

"Yeah." Her smile faded. "And he didn't even complain about it. I guess it's really boring at home during the day."

Could Randy be the one slipping the counterfeit bills into the cash box? He didn't fit the profile of a counterfeiter, but he was a troubled kid who'd been acting out a lot lately.

A wash of relief spilled over Seth. Maybe he could still trust his instincts. Maybe his gut had been right—Kat wasn't involved.

He'd skip out of the office early and have a little talk with Randy.

HALFWAY THROUGH THEIR HOURS on Saturday morning, Kat dropped off a patient folder at the front desk and frowned at the untouched coffee cup sitting at the back of the counter. "Where's Jenna?"

"She never showed up." Barb tightened her lips. "I tried calling her house, but no one answered."

"Try her again," Kat said, fear stirring. "Keep trying until you get hold of her."

"She probably overslept," Barb said, reaching for the phone.

"I don't know." Annie looked from Barb to Kat, chewing a pen. "Jenna's pretty reliable."

Kat glanced at the patients in the waiting room. "Let me know when you get in touch with her."

Just before noon, as Kat was saying goodbye to a patient, the door to the clinic burst open and Randy hurried in, pulling Jenna behind him. "Mom," he yelled. "Get Dr. Mac. Quick."

Kat squeezed past her elderly patient and ran into the waiting room. Randy had his arm wrapped around Jenna's shoulder, and the girl held a protective arm across her belly. Her hair was damp and uncombed—as if she'd just gotten out of the shower—and there was a bruise on her cheek.

"Oh, no." She reached for Jenna, smoothing the hair away from the bruise, noticing the way the girl was hunched over. "Randy, bring her back to the exam room."

Barb and Annie watched with shocked faces as Jenna shuffled down the hall and into a room. Kat closed the door firmly behind them and helped Jenna onto the table.

"What happened?" she asked as she examined Jenna's face.

"Her parents found out she was pregnant," Randy said. He tightened his arm around Jenna's shoulder, pulling her closer to him.

"Did they hurt you, Jenna?" Kat asked, grabbing the girl's hands.

Tears ran down her face as Jenna slowly shook her head.

"Were you with Jenna when she was hurt?" Kat asked Randy.

"No. She called me from her friend's house. Craig drove me to get her, and we brought her here."

"Jenna." Kat waited until the girl looked at her again. "Tell me where you were hurt." She glanced at the arm Jenna still held across her abdomen. "Is it your belly?"

"Yes," Jenna whispered. "I fell down the stairs."

"Okay, let's take a look at you." She eased the girl's coat off and unbuckled her overalls, then helped her lie down on the exam table. Randy stood next to Jenna, holding her hand, watching as Kat gently palpated her uterus. A bruise darkened the skin across the small bump. "Any bleeding?" Kat asked.

Jenna shook her head. Kat pressed the wand of the ultrasound machine against the girl's abdomen and drew a ragged breath of relief when the baby's heartbeat filled the room. "So far, so good."

She finished her exam and treated the abrasion on Jenna's face, then she helped the girl get dressed again. "Okay, Jenna. Randy. We need to talk."

Jenna started crying again and Randy put his arm around her. She looked terrified, and Randy looked helpless and baffled. "Jenna, can you tell me what happened?" Kat asked.

Jenna sniffled a few times, then pressed her hands against her abdomen. "My mother came into the bathroom when I was getting out of the shower. I thought I had locked the door, but she saw me. Saw my belly." Tears leaked out of her eyes. "She freaked out and started yelling at me."

"Then what?" Kat rubbed her hand.

"She called my dad, and he started yelling, too. Then they told me to get out. They said I was a bad influence on my sisters and brother."

"How did you get hurt?" Kat asked.

Jenna sniffed. "I was running down the stairs and I slipped." She swiped at her nose. "On one of my little brother's cars. I fell down a few steps."

"What did your parents do then?" Kat asked.

"Nothing. I went to my friend's house and called Randy."

"Self-righteous bastards," Kat muttered under her breath. She'd never liked Jenna's parents.

"What did you say?" Jenna asked.

"I said we'll figure out what to do," Kat answered. "Hold on a minute. I'm going to get you a drink of water."

Kat slipped out the door and rested against it for a moment, trying to compose herself. Seth stepped out from behind the front desk. "Kat. What do you need?"

"I need to knock some sense into a couple of so-called adults," she said fiercely.

He wrapped his arm around her shoulder and steered her toward her office, where he closed the door behind her. "What's up?"

"A mess," she said, stepping into his arms and holding him tightly. "A complete and total disaster."

He held her close, pressing her head into his neck, and his steady heartbeat and familiar scent calmed her. She tightened her arms around him, reluctant to let go. To leave the comfort she found there.

She'd never looked to a man for comfort before. She'd never relied on anyone but herself. Never wanted to.

She stepped away from him. "Will you call Brady Morgan at the sheriff's department? Ask him to come by."

Seth's hands tightened on her arms. "Is it Randy? Is he in trouble?"

She sighed. "They're both in trouble."

He held her away from him, assessing her. "This has something to do with those prenatal vitamins, doesn't it? Jenna's his girlfriend. She's pregnant."

He was too quick. What else did he see when he looked at her? "Just call Brady, okay?"

She got a glass of water and headed back to the exam room, leaving Seth in her office. Closing the door behind her, she pulled the chair next to the exam table. "Sit down, Randy," she said. She looked from Randy's scared face to Jenna's bruised one. "Randy, you have to tell your mother what's going on. You need her help."

"I can't," Randy said.

"Why not?" Kat took a deep breath, hoping she looked calmer than she felt.

The boy glanced at Jenna's belly. "She'll be upset," he muttered.

"Of course she'll be upset. But she loves you, and you need her help. You two have a lot to deal with."

Randy and Jenna looked at each other, their eyes fearful. But Kat also saw resignation. And relief. They were tired of carrying this burden alone. Kat stood up. "I have one more patient to see. You two decide what you want to say to Randy's mom. I'll be right back."

Barb and Annie rushed over when they saw her. "Is Jenna okay? What's going on?" Barb demanded.

"Let me see the last patient," Kat said. "Then we'll sort this out." She squeezed Barb's arm. "Hang in there," she murmured.

As she took the last file from the holder on the exam-room door, Seth emerged from the office. "I got hold of Morgan," he said quietly. "He'll be here in fifteen minutes."

"Thank you," she said. She glanced at her watch. "We're closing in a few minutes. Would you stick around?"

"I'm not going anywhere."

She nodded, then opened the exam-room door. Mary Boehmer needed a refill of her prescriptions. Kat examined her and wrote the script, countering her curious questions with a smile. When the woman finally left the clinic, Kat took a deep breath. Seth, Annie and Barb watched her from behind the desk.

"Okay. Hold on for a few minutes. I'll be right back," she said to them.

Stepping into the room with Randy and Jenna, she was surprised to find Jenna dry-eyed and Randy looking grim but calm. "It looks like you two have done some talking," Kat said.

"We're going to tell my mom," Randy answered. "Maybe Jenna can stay with us."

"I'm glad you're going to tell Barb. But I'm not sure it's a good idea for Jenna to stay with you right now."

"How come?" Randy asked, but she saw his flicker of relief.

"There are some legal reasons," Kat said. "Jenna is a minor." She took the girl's hand again. "Remember I told you about that shelter when you came in to see me?" she said.

Jenna nodded. "Is that where you think I should go?"

"Yes, Jenna. I can drive you there after we get this all sorted out, if you like."

The girl darted a glance at Randy. "I'd rather stay with Randy."

"I know you would, sweetheart," Kat said. "But the woman who runs the shelter is a social worker. She can help you with the decisions you have to make. Randy can visit you whenever you like."

"Okay," she whispered. She crossed her arms over her belly and more tears dripped down her face. "You can take me there."

"Do you want to talk to your mom now, Randy?" Kat asked.

"I guess." He swallowed.

"Will you stay with us, Dr. Mac?" Jenna asked.

"You both want me here?" Kat looked from one teen to the other.

They both nodded.

"Okay. I'll stay while you tell her." Kat opened the door and called, "Barb? Could you come in here?"

When her receptionist walked in, she grabbed her son. "Are you okay?"

"I'm fine, Mom," Randy said, but he hugged his mother.

Barb turned to Jenna, her arm around Randy. Her stiff demeanor softened when she saw the bruise on Jenna's face. "What happened, honey?"

"Sit down, Barb," Kat said, pushing her stool toward the woman. "Randy and Jenna have something to tell you."

"What?" Barb asked, plopping down on the chair. "What's going on?"

Kat squeezed her friend's shoulder, wishing there was more she could do to help her.

Randy eased away from his mother and took Jenna's hand. His knuckles were white and his Adam's apple bobbed. Finally, after one panicked glance at Kat, he said, "Mom, Jenna is pregnant. And I'm the father."

CHAPTER SIXTEEN

"WHAT?" BARB'S FACE BLANCHED and she looked from her son to Jenna. "Is this a joke?"

"I wouldn't joke about that, Mom," Randy said sharply. "Jeez!"

"You're pregnant?" Barb asked Jenna, her gaze going to the curve of the girl's belly, outlined by her overalls.

"Yes, Mrs. Morris."

"Randy," Barb whispered, staring at Jenna's belly, her eyes filling with tears. "How could you let this happen?"

"We didn't mean for Jenna to get pregnant," the boy retorted, but he swallowed again. "We used condoms. We're not stupid and irresponsible."

Barb stared from her son to Jenna and bit her lip. "What happened to your face, Jenna?"

Kat laid her hand on the girl's shoulder. "Jenna's parents found out about the pregnancy today. They threw her out, and she tripped on the stairs as she was leaving. Randy picked her up and brought her here."

"You fell on the stairs?" Barb sucked in a breath. "The baby?"

"The baby is all right so far," Kat reassured her.

Barb scrubbed her face with her hands. "We were going to have the sex talk this weekend," she said to Randy. "I guess it's too late for that."

"Jeez, Mom," Randy muttered, turning red. "I'm not a baby."

"No, you're *having* a baby," Barb retorted. "So don't sneer at me. We should have talked about sex long before now."

Kat's heart ached for all of them. "You and Randy and Jenna have a lot of things to talk about, but here's what we're thinking. Jenna said she'd go to Zoe McInnes's shelter in Spruce Lake. I know Zoe and I can vouch for her. She'll take good care of Jenna."

"She'll be all by herself," Randy said.

"There are several women in the shelter right now, and she'll see a lot of me," Kat answered. "I'm the shelter's on-call physician. I'm there every Wednesday night. And you can visit her anytime you like. Jenna won't be alone."

"What if the shelter doesn't have room?" Jenna asked.

"I was there a few nights ago. They have plenty of room."

"Okay." Barb sounded shell-shocked.

"Brady Morgan should be here soon," Kat said. "I'm going to have him take you back to your house so you can get what you need. All right, Jenna?"

The girl snapped her head up, terrified. "No. I can't go back there."

"Yes, you can. You're a minor, Jenna. Your parents can't throw you out of the house, but you shouldn't stay there right now. Brady will make sure your parents don't give you a hard time while you get your belongings."

"I don't need anything." Jenna's eyes were wide with fright.

"You'll be more comfortable with your own things," Kat said gently.

"I'll go with you," Randy said.

He looked queasy, but he stood close beside her.

"That's very brave of you, Randy," Kat said. "I'm proud of you for offering, and I'm sure your mom is, too. But that's probably not a good idea."

Barb straightened her shoulders. "I'll go with you, Jenna. Your parents won't bully you if I'm there."

Not if they knew what was good for them, Kat thought with her first smile of the morning.

"I'll see if Brady is here yet."

Outside the exam-room door, Kat found Seth talking in a low voice to Brady. He broke off when he saw her. "I told Annie she could go home. I hope that's okay."

"You must have read my mind. Thank you." It was scary how easily she and Seth had meshed. Would they mesh as well in other areas of their lives?

Pushing the thought from her mind, she explained to Brady what she needed.

"No problem." A muscle in his jaw tightened. "Poor kid."

"Bring her back here when you're finished." She gave the police officer a hug. "Thanks, Brady."

As Randy, Jenna and Barb emerged from the exam room, Randy said, "I'm going with you, Jenna. Don't argue. I'm not letting you face them alone."

"Randy." Seth stepped toward him, and alarm tightened the boy's face. Seth laid his hand on Randy's shoulder. "You're standing up like a man," he said. "I'm proud of you, and I'm sure your mom is, too."

He glanced at Barb, who started crying again. "He's right, Randy. I *am* proud of you."

Randy looked from Seth to his mom and stood a little taller. "Thanks."

"But you're still waiting in the car," Barb added.

Brady ushered Barb, Jenna and Randy out the door, and silence descended. Dust danced in the sunlight that streamed through the windows, and Kat reached for Seth's hand.

"Thank you. Randy needed to hear that from another man."

"It's true. Not a lot of kids his age would step up to the plate like he has. He even risked getting arrested to get her vitamins." He shook his head. "Why didn't he just buy them for her?"

"There were girls he knew at the drugstore," Kat told him. "He didn't want them to see him buying prenatal vitamins. He knew they'd tell everyone at school."

He shifted his hand, twined their fingers together. "How far along is she?"

"Four months."

"And no one noticed until now? Her parents didn't realize she was pregnant? Didn't they ever *look* at her, for God's sake?"

"People see what they expect to see," Kat sighed. "Her parents weren't expecting her to be pregnant. She wore baggy clothes and probably stayed in her room a lot."

"What's the plan?" he asked. He smoothed her hair away from her face and smiled. "I know you have one. You're good at taking care of people."

She tried to smile back and failed. "I'm taking her to a shelter."

"In Sturgeon Falls?"

"No, in Spruce Lake. A town about thirty minutes away. It would be tough for her to stay in school here. Better to start somewhere that no one knows her. The kids will still stare, but they won't be kids she's grown up with."

"Can I go with you to the shelter?"

He stood in a beam of sunlight that bounced off his dark hair and shimmered around him like gold. His brown eyes were golden in the sun, as well. He was solid and strong.

She hadn't been looking for a man to lean on. She hadn't been interested in sharing her burdens. But she'd found one just the same. "I'd like that," she said. "Very much."

His eyes were knowing as he pulled her close. "You don't want to need anyone, do you?" he murmured into her hair. "You're capable, smart and strong. You can handle anything."

"That's not true," she whispered. "I need you. I don't know how it happened, but there it is."

"I need you, too, Kat. And it scares the hell out of me."

She eased away from him. "We're quite the pair, aren't we?"

He shoved his hand through his hair and didn't quite meet her eyes. "Yeah. We are."

A car's tires crunched on the gravel in the parking lot, and she peered out the window. "They're back."

"That didn't take long."

She watched Jenna climb out of the patrol car, holding a battered suitcase. The girl looked desolate. "I guess there wasn't much for her to get at home."

SEVERAL HOURS LATER, as they drove away from Spruce Lake and the Safe Harbor Women's Shelter, Kat murmured, "Thank you, Seth."

"I didn't do much." He stared out the window.

"Yeah, you did. You were great with Randy. I heard you tell him you'd pick him up after school Monday and drive him to the shelter. That's a big deal."

Seth glanced at her and smiled, but there were shadows in his eyes. "I've got a lot of time on my hands."

"Bored with working at the clinic already?" she teased.

Instead of smiling, he shrugged. "I've set up the system. Barb and Annie can handle it now."

"You're not going to come in every day?" She was surprised how disappointed she was.

"I'm getting in everyone's way. I'll check in once in a while."

It almost sounded like goodbye. Had he made his

decision? Was he going to sign the papers and let her adopt Regan, then disappear from their lives?

Kat wanted him to sign the papers, but she didn't want him to disappear. She wanted him to be part of their lives. To watch Regan grow up.

She pressed on the accelerator. That was fantasyland. Seth's life was in Washington, doing his job at the Secret Service. Whether or not he signed the adoption papers, he wasn't going to stick around Sturgeon Falls.

"Why do you look so sad?" Seth asked.

She tightened her grip on the steering wheel. "I always get a little sad on the way home from the shelter. There's so much unhappiness there," she said. The shelter had nothing to do with her mood today.

"There's also hope," he said. "Something a lot of those women and kids haven't had much of in the past."

"Do you know that from personal experience?" she asked softly.

He stared straight ahead for so long that she didn't think he'd answer. Finally he said, "No. We never went to a shelter. My mother didn't want to admit she needed help."

"I'm sorry."

"It was a long time ago." He glanced at her. "How did you get involved with that shelter? It's a long drive for you."

His change of subject wasn't subtle, but she let it go. He'd opened a tiny door, and maybe if she didn't push, he'd open it a little more. "Zoe sent a letter to all the doctors in the area, looking for someone to treat her patients. I volunteered. That was before I had Regan."

"Does it take a lot of time?"

"I go one night a week, more often if I'm needed. My parents or Hayley watch Regan those nights. All three of them love the time together."

"Is Jenna going to be all right?"

"I hope so." She sent up a quick prayer for the girl. "I don't like that she fell onto her abdomen. The next several days are critical, and Zoe will keep a close eye on her."

"You take care of everyone," he murmured, smoothing his hand over her head. "Who takes care of you?"

His fingers slid through her hair and caressed her scalp, making her shiver. "I don't need anyone to take care of me," she managed to say. She tried to focus on the road in front of her, but she could concentrate on nothing but his hand gliding over her scalp. Her pulse pounded, and she sucked in a breath when his fingers found it and lingered.

"Are you sure of that, Kat?" He cupped her neck in his palm, covering her leaping pulse. "Sure you don't need anyone?"

She needed to pay attention to her driving. Dragging her attention away from the play of his hand on her skin, she said, "I don't confuse lust with need."

"Is that what this is? Lust?" He stroked his hand over her neck, and her pulse leaped again.

It was need, and that scared her. Badly. "I can't concentrate when you're touching me."

He skimmed his finger down her neck. "That's good to know," he said, his voice low and intimate. He took his hand away. "I can wait. But not too long."

She wanted to snatch it back. She ached for his touch.

She was in so much trouble.

She turned down County TT, sighing with relief when the familiar landmarks flashed past in the dusk. Thank goodness they were almost home.

As she turned into her driveway and reached for the ignition key, he put his hand on hers. "Before we go inside, are you sure Regan is going to be okay?" he asked.

She shot him a surprised glance. "Why do you ask now?"

"Because once we close that door, I'm not going to be thinking about Regan."

She drew in a sharp breath, battling the need to forget everything else and lose herself in Seth's sensual promise. "I called Charlotte before we left the shelter. Regan seems to be having a great time. She and Hayley are going to make popcorn and watch a movie."

He stroked his hand down her hair again. "That's good." He fumbled with the band holding her braid in place, freeing the wild curls she tried to keep tamed. "You have beautiful hair," he said, letting it curl around his fingers. "Why do you keep it hidden?"

"It gets in the way," she said, her voice ragged. "It's too hard to control."

She heard his sharp intake of breath. "Out of control is good." He speared both hands into the mass of curls, drew her closer. "I like out of control."

He slanted his mouth across hers, and his hands trembled against her head. His lips slid across hers, tasting. Exploring. He nipped at her lower lip, and she cupped her hands around his face and pressed her mouth to his.

He stilled for a moment, then groaned deep in his throat. His mouth moved over hers, possessing and claiming. When he stroked his tongue along the seam of her mouth, she moaned and he swept inside.

Desire rushed through her, heating her skin, making her throb. Her breasts swelled and pressed against her bra, unbearably sensitive. She reached toward him, desperate to feel his body against hers.

He pulled her closer and she got tangled in the

gearshift. She tugged at her jacket, trying to yank it out of the way, but it was stuck. Finally he eased the pressure of his kiss, brushing his mouth over her lips, her cheeks, her eyes.

"Damn bucket seats," he said, continuing to kiss her. "Where's a good bench seat when you need one?"

She forced her eyes open to find him smiling down at her. "I haven't made out in a car since I was seventeen." He bit down lightly on the tendon in her neck, and she shuddered. "I forgot how much fun it is."

He eased her away from him and tugged at her jacket. Moments later, it fell open and he shoved it down her arms. "Too many clothes," he whispered.

He cupped her breast through her blouse. "Seth," she whispered, reaching for him. As he kissed her, he fumbled with the buttons, and cool air feathered across her chest.

"Black lace," he breathed as he stared down at her bra. "You're killing me, Kat." He pressed his mouth to her breast through the bra and her nipple tightened almost painfully. As he nuzzled her, he trailed a finger down her chest to her belly, making her skin jump.

As he fumbled with the clasp of her bra, she reached for the button on his jeans. Her fingers brushed the bulge of his erection, and he sucked in a breath. She brushed him again, feeling him surge against her hand. "Is this what you do when you make out in a car?" she whispered as she opened his waistband. "Check out each other's underwear?"

"Oh, yeah," he groaned. "But you're not looking closely enough."

She grinned as she slid her hand around him. "I like the silk."

"You mentioned that before," he gasped. "I paid attention."

She squeezed gently and he arched into her hand. "I like a man who listens to women."

He opened the clasp of her bra and filled his hands with her. Her hand tightened on him as he brushed her nipples with his thumbs.

As she fumbled with his shorts, trying to pull them down, he took her hands in his. "Stop, Kat." He kissed her palms. "Or I'm going to embarrass myself." He kissed her again, then let her go as he buttoned his jeans. Then he pulled the edges of her blouse together, brushing his hand over her nipples one last time. "I forgot the drawbacks to making out in a car."

His face was taut and his eyes were dark. His chest rose and fell, and his hands shook as he drew her jacket over her shoulders.

"Let's go in the house," she whispered.

CHAPTER SEVENTEEN

KAT LOCKED THE DOOR then turned to Seth, dropping her jacket on the floor. He backed her against the wall and fastened his mouth to hers, kissing her with a desperation that matched her own. She twined one leg around his and tried to pull him closer.

Her blouse and bra hung open, and her bare breasts pressed against his flannel shirt. He slid his hands down her back, touching each bump of her spine, lingering on the flare of her hips. She framed his face with her hands and held him to her as she kissed him.

Without taking his mouth from hers, he shoved her blouse and bra off her shoulders, leaving her naked from the waist up. "Beautiful," he murmured as he weighed her breasts in his hands, thumbing her nipples. "I need to taste you."

He lowered his head and took one tip in his mouth, swirling his tongue around it. When he suckled gently, she shuddered and tightened her grip on him. If she hadn't, she would have slid to the floor.

"Bedroom," she managed to gasp, sagging against him. "Now."

He took her hand and led her down the hall to her bedroom. Dim light from the moon flickered over the silk bedspread and mounds of pillows that covered it. He shoved them out of the way, then laid her down on the sheets.

He didn't take his eyes off her as he got out of his shirt and his jeans. Before he dropped them on the floor, he took a flat packet from his pocket and set it on the night table. She fumbled in the drawer and withdrew a box of condoms. "I have more."

He grinned. "You really are an optimist, aren't you?"

"Just hopeful," she answered, and he laughed.

"I hope I don't disappoint you."

"Not a chance." She smoothed her hands over his chest, the dark hair coarse and springy beneath her palms. Propping herself on her elbows, she teased his flat nipple with her tongue.

Sucking in a breath, he knelt beside her and tugged off her pants, then smoothed his hand over the scrap of black lace that was all she wore. "Sexy Kat." He nuzzled her belly. "I need you so much."

She wound her arms around his neck and pulled him close, kissing him as he eased his fingers beneath the edge of the lacy underwear. He stroked his finger over her once, then again as she trembled in his arms.

Trailing his mouth over her chest, then her belly, he pulled the lace down her legs and pressed his mouth between her thighs.

She exploded, crying his name, and he slipped inside her. Wrapping her legs around his waist, she kissed him as the tension built again. When he shuddered and thrust into her one last time, she bowed off the bed and came once more.

SEVERAL HOURS LATER, Kat sprawled on top of him, her skin sheened with sweat, her breath coming in ragged gasps. He threaded his fingers through her hair and pressed her closer. "Don't move," he whispered. "Don't ever move again."

She touched his face, her fingers rasping against his stubble. "I couldn't move if I wanted to. Which I don't."

"Good." He stroked the length of her back and over her hip, savoring the softness of her skin and the way she snuggled closer as he touched her. Her heart beat against his, its frantic pace gradually slowing, and her skin cooled beneath his hand. She was perfect, and their lovemaking had been equally perfect.

Nothing had ever felt so right.

He was terrified he would lose her.

As soon as he was certain Randy was responsible for the counterfeit bills, he'd tell Kat everything—

why he was really here, how he'd been using her and Regan. He'd beg her forgiveness. He didn't want to go back to Washington and never see her again. Her or Regan. He couldn't bear it.

His mind danced around the alternative. He didn't want to think about that right now. It was enough to know he wasn't ready to leave them. He didn't think Kat wanted him to leave, either. They could start from there.

Kat reached down and pulled the blankets over them. "You cold?" he murmured.

"Little."

Her face was buried in his neck, and he turned to kiss her hair. "I'll keep you warm."

He felt her smile. "You've been doing a good job," she said. Her hand fumbled for the package of condoms on the night table. "But they're not all gone."

"I'm pacing myself. I don't want to run out before morning."

Her laugh tickled his neck. "That would be very bad."

As he drifted off to sleep holding Kat close, his mind wandered to the future. To falling asleep with Kat in his arms every night. Waking up with her every morning.

He had a strict rule about the future—he never thought about it. Maybe it was time to change the rules.

A SHARP RINGING JERKED HIM OUT of sleep. Kat shot up in the bed next to him and fumbled for the phone in the dark. "Hello?"

He heard her breathing as she listened. "I'll be right there," she finally said.

"That was my brother," she said as she swung out of bed. She slid the scrap of black lace back on and reached for a T-shirt. "Regan had a nightmare and she wants to come home."

He grabbed his jeans and tugged them on, then shrugged into his shirt. "I'll come with you."

"You don't have to," she said.

He stilled. "Would you rather I didn't?"

She glanced at the clock—3:15 a.m. Far too late to say they'd been on a date.

"I'll wait here," he said quickly.

She reached for his hand. "I'd like you to come with me," she said softly. "If you're sure it wouldn't bother you."

He didn't want to face her brother in the middle of the night. But he wanted to be there for Regan. "I'll be ready to go as soon as I find my shoes."

They didn't see another car on the way. When they pulled up in front of a tidy white house, the living-room light was on.

He held Kat's hand as they ran up the steps. A woman with long blond hair opened the front door before they reached it. She held Regan in her arms. "Here they are, sweetie," she murmured into Regan's hair.

Regan lifted her head. Her eyes were swollen and her nose was red. She looked from him to Kat. "Seth? Why are you here?"

He felt himself flush. "I wanted to make sure you were all right," he answered.

The blonde raised her eyebrows at Kat as Regan scrambled into Kat's arms. She buried her face in Kat's neck as they walked into the house.

"Charlotte, Dylan, this is Seth Anderson," Kat murmured. "Seth, Charlotte Burns and Dylan Smith." A man in rumpled sleep pants gave him a sleepy wave, then handed him Regan's Tinkerbell suitcase.

"I'll call you tomorrow," Charlotte said, stroking Regan's hair. She glanced at Seth. "When we have time to talk. You need to get her home."

They said goodbye quickly and buckled Regan into her car seat. She was half-asleep already as Kat started her car and headed back the way they'd come.

SETH FELT A SMALL HAND TOUCH his face the next morning. He opened his eyes and Regan pulled her hand away as if she'd been burned.

"Hey, Regan," he said, sitting up. He stretched, trying to loosen muscles cramped from sleeping on a too-short couch.

"Why are you sleeping on the couch? Are you having a sleepover with us?"

"I guess I am," he said, wrapping the blanket around his waist and reaching for his jeans and shirt. "I wanted to make sure you were all right this morning."

She gave him a puzzled look. "Why wouldn't I be all right?"

Kat came out of the bedroom, tying a sash around a long green silk robe. He let himself savor the sight for a long moment, then he looked at Regan again. "Because…"

"Because he never heard about your fishing trip yesterday," Kat interrupted smoothly. "He wanted to make sure no fish nibbled on you."

Regan giggled and Seth's heart contracted. "Aunt Charlotte wouldn't let the fish nibble me. She said I'm her favorite niece."

"I can see why." Seth looked at her tousled hair and her SpongeBob pajamas and the creases in her face from her pillow and realized he was in love. Kat sat down on the couch, brushing his leg with hers, and his heart turned over again. He was in love with both of them.

What if they didn't love him back?

"Come here and tell us about the fishing," Kat said, pulling Regan into her lap.

As Regan chattered about the boat and the fish

they'd caught, Seth's heart creaked open. It had been a very long time since he'd let anyone inside.

SETH SAT OUTSIDE Sturgeon Falls High School in his rental car and watched teenagers pour out of the building. He'd called Barb on Sunday and told her he'd pick Randy up from school. He needed to talk to the boy without anyone interrupting.

Randy was one of the last kids out of the school. His backpack was slung over one shoulder and his shoelaces were untied. He scanned the cars lined up at the curb until he spotted Seth.

He hurried to the car and slid into the passenger seat. "Hey, Mr. Anderson," he said. "Thanks for taking me to see Jenna."

"Hi, Randy," Seth answered as he pulled out of the parking lot. "Glad to do it." He drove to a park he'd scouted out earlier in the day. The parking lot was deserted, and he smiled grimly. He wanted Randy to be a little nervous.

Randy gave him a bewildered look. "What are we doing here, man? I thought we were going to Spruce Lake to see Jenna."

"We are. I need to talk to you first, and I didn't want to be interrupted."

The boy slumped down in the seat. "Are you going to yell at me about the baby, too?"

"Of course not. And I doubt your mom was yelling at you over the weekend."

"She was crying," Randy muttered. "That's worse."

"Your mom's scared for you."

Randy looked at him out of the corner of his eye. "Why would *she* be scared? I'm the one who messed up."

Seth sighed. "You messed up, but you're paying for it. Think how your mom feels. Parents want to fix things for their kids, and she can't fix this."

"Do you have any kids?"

"Yes. I do."

Randy slumped in the seat again. "So can we go see Jenna now?"

"Not just yet. I need to ask you some questions, and you need to answer me truthfully." Seth had thought for a long time about the best way to approach Randy. He pulled out his badge and laid it on the seat.

Randy's eyes widened. "Are you a cop?"

"I'm in the Secret Service," Seth answered.

"Yeah?" The teen straightened. "That's cool. You guard the president and sh...ah, stuff like that?"

"That's one of the things the Secret Service does." He folded his badge into his wallet and put it away. "But we investigate crimes, too." He turned so he could see Randy's entire face. "Randy, have you been putting hundred-dollar bills into the cash box at your mom's office?"

Randy's eyes shifted to the left and he wouldn't meet Seth's gaze. "Where would I get a hundred-dollar bill, man? I don't even have a job."

"That's what I need to know. Where you're getting the bills. And why you're putting them into the cash box."

Randy wiped his hands down his thighs. "I don't know what you're talking about." One of his legs began to bounce.

"Those bills are counterfeit. Passing counterfeit bills is a crime, and you could go to prison for a long time," Seth said.

Randy's face went white. "Counterfeit? No way. He never…" He clamped his mouth shut.

"He never told you they were phony bills?" Seth asked. "Who's he?"

"I can't tell you. I promised." Randy swallowed and his Adam's apple bobbed.

Seth leaned forward. "I like you, Randy, and I like your mom. I don't want to arrest you. But you need to tell me who gave you that money."

"Is my mom in trouble?"

"Was she involved in this?"

"No! She didn't know anything about it."

"Then she doesn't have anything to worry about. But you do."

"I'll give the money back," Randy said. "I got to keep twenty dollars every time I changed one. I only spent a little of it," he said wildly.

"We'll worry about the money later. Right now I need to know who gave you those bills." He watched Randy squirm, but the boy didn't say anything. "Randy, loyalty is a good thing, and so is protecting your friends. But this isn't the time for it. This guy is using you. You don't owe him a thing."

"He'll be so pissed off," Randy said, his eyes everywhere but on Seth's face. He reached for a door handle, and Seth put his hand on Randy's arm.

"Is he a friend of yours? Are you afraid he'll hurt you?" He waited, but Randy didn't look at him. "We'll protect you, if that's what you're worried about."

"What about my mom?"

"Her, too."

"It's complicated," Randy muttered.

"Yeah, it always is. Take all the time you need to explain." He stretched out as if he had all the time in the world. "You want to do the right thing, Randy. I know you do. I saw you with Jenna. I know what kind of kid you are. Now I need your help."

CHAPTER EIGHTEEN

REGAN CLUTCHED KAT'S HAND tightly as she slid out of the car, staring at the flashing neon pirate holding a pizza. "Is this the place?"

"This is Cheesy Pete's." Kat checked the birthday present that Regan hugged to her chest to make sure the card hadn't fallen off, then re-clipped her barrettes. "Are you ready?"

Regan nodded without taking her eyes off the pirate, and Kat smiled. "Then let's go."

As they started walking toward the restaurant, Regan looked behind her. "Where's Seth?"

"I'm right here," Seth said, coming around the car. He was trying not to limp, and Kat sighed. He was determined that Regan not see him using his cane. "I can't wait to check this place out."

"Ginny said they have games and rides. And pizza and cake." Her eyes grew wide. "As much as we want."

"Wow. I wish I could stay." Seth watched Regan,

a bemused look on his face, and Kat stifled a laugh. Clearly he'd never seen a child in the throes of birthday-party mania.

Regan nodded vigorously. "I want to have *my* birthday at Cheesy Pete's."

"Next summer is a long time from now," Kat said.

"I know who I want to invite, too." She sounded very definite. Then she glanced at Seth. "Are you going to be here for my birthday, Seth?"

His face stilled and he shoved his hands into his pockets. "I hope so," he said without looking at her.

"Me, too," Regan said, oblivious to the sudden tension.

Seth opened the door and they walked into a wall of noise. Video games beeped and clanged and roared, children screamed and calliope music drifted from another room. He looked horrified.

Kat grinned. "We're only dropping her off. Suck it up."

"This is fun?" He stared around as if he'd just discovered an alien species.

"It is if you're six."

She saw a sign for Ginny's party and steered Regan into a large room decorated with balloons and streamers. The plastic tablecloth was pink and there were pink tiaras and wands by each place. Regan's eyes got even wider.

"Look," she whispered. "Crowns."

Kat bent and kissed her, and Regan hardly noticed. She was too busy staring around the room. "Seth and I will be back to pick you up when the party's over," she said. "Okay, Regan?"

Regan nodded. "Yeah," she said. Then she spotted Ginny and darted away.

A harried-looking woman came up. "You must be Regan's mom and dad," she said. "I'm Sue Goodson."

"Nice to meet you, Sue," Kat said. "I'm Kat, and this is Seth." *Regan's mom and dad.* The words were bittersweet, and she glanced at Seth to see if he'd heard them. He was watching Regan, who was carefully setting her present on a table with several others.

"You have my cell number, right?" Kat asked, and Sue nodded. "We'll be back in two hours."

"Great. See you then."

As they walked out of the restaurant into the early evening light, the doors cut off the noise. "Who knew the ninth circle of hell involved pizza and pirates?" Seth said with a shudder as he slid into the car.

"The kids love it."

"And she wants to go back there for her own birthday?" He grimaced.

Kat waited until they were back on County TT.

"There are Cheesy Pete's all over the country," she said without looking at him.

He turned into her driveway and switched the car off. The engine ticked as it cooled down. "I don't want to take her away from you, Kat."

"Then don't." She gripped her handbag tightly. "Sign the adoption papers."

"I can't leave her." He closed his eyes. "Or you."

Hope bloomed inside her, but she was afraid to grab it. "What are you saying, Seth?"

"I care about both of you," he said. "And I don't know what to do about it."

She turned to face him, her heart racing painfully fast. They lived in different parts of the country, had different outlooks on life, different goals. None of it seemed important compared to what she felt for him. What she hoped he felt for her. "Do we have to do anything right now? Can't we just see what happens?"

"That doesn't bother you?" he asked. "To leave things hanging?"

She hated not having anything settled, but she knew how much his admission had cost him. "I'm trying really hard not to back you into a corner."

"Thank you, Kat." He cupped her face in his palm, leaned toward her and kissed her. "I know what I want to happen right now," he murmured. "How much time do we have before we pick Regan up?"

She glanced at her watch. "An hour and forty-five minutes."

He gave her a slow, wicked smile. "Seems like two people could accomplish a lot in that much time."

She fumbled for the door. "I'll race you to the house."

KAT GLANCED AT THE CLOCK and reluctantly sat up. "We need to get going," she said as she picked up one sock from the floor. She followed the trail to the front door, retrieving the rest of her clothes as she went.

Seth was right behind her, pulling on his shirt. "Is this what parents do?" he asked with a grin. "Sneak a quickie while their kids are at a birthday party?"

She looped her arms around his neck. "A quickie?" She trailed her lips down his throat. "I thought it was slow and thorough."

He kissed her hungrily, let her go with a groan. "Be careful or we'll be late for Regan. We don't want anyone to think we're bad parents."

She grabbed her jacket and headed out the door. *Parents.* He'd used the word twice in less than a minute. Hope shimmered again, and she ignored it for the second time. She couldn't afford to hope.

But she couldn't resist pushing a little. As they drove toward the restaurant, she asked, "Is that what we are, Seth? Regan's parents?"

"Yeah," he answered after a long pause. "I guess we are." The car rolled to a stop at a red light and he looked over at her. "Kat, I..."

"Yes?" she prompted when he hesitated. He appeared tense and uncomfortable. Nervous. Then the light changed and he pressed the accelerator. She was certain he was relieved.

"Have you talked to Jenna recently?" he asked.

He hadn't been going to ask her about Jenna, but she let it go. "I talked to Zoe yesterday," she said. "Jenna is bleeding a little, and Zoe is taking her to an ob-gyn. I'm worried."

"You did all you could for her."

"I know. But I want to do more. I know how alone Jenna feels." Anger flashed through her. "Jenna's mother should be taking her to the doctor. Not a stranger at a shelter."

"Not all mothers care about their kids. At least Jenna has you."

His voice was haunted and she turned to look at him. "Did your mother care about you?"

"My mother disappeared when I was nine."

"What happened to her?"

He shrugged. "I have no idea. She was gone when I woke up one morning. The guy she was living with called the county and they put me in a foster home."

She took his hand. "Your mother left without you?" No wonder he didn't want to talk about the past.

"I never heard from her again. But I'm not sure she left."

The hair rose on the back of Kat's neck. "What do you mean?"

"The guy she was living with was a mean SOB. I wondered if he'd killed her and dumped her body somewhere."

"Did you tell the police?"

"I tried. But the guy was a buddy of the police chief. He wasn't interested in what I had to say."

"That's horrible." She pressed his hand against her cheek. "Did you ever go back and try to figure out what happened?"

"Once. I didn't get anywhere." He tightened his grip on her hand. "I was just the foster kid who'd kicked around from home to home, causing trouble wherever I went. As soon as I made noises about my mother, I was pegged as a troublemaker. Nothing had changed when I went back after college. Small towns have long memories."

"Thank you for telling me," she whispered. No wonder he'd been so insistent on making sure Regan was well cared for. He didn't want his child to end up in the system the way he had.

"I don't like to talk about it," he muttered.

But he had. For her.

Two days later, Kat was standing at the front desk talking to Annie about a patient when the door burst open and Randy rushed in. He looked past all three of them. "Is Mr. Anderson here?" he asked, breathless.

"He's at the gym," Kat said. "Why?"

"I need to talk to him. Like right now."

"Randy?" Barb stood up. "What's wrong?"

"Nothing, Mom," Randy said, but he wouldn't meet her eyes. Instead, he looked at Kat. "Could you call him, Dr. Mac? Ask him to come over here?"

"He's supposed to come by in an hour or so. Can it wait that long?"

"No!" Randy touched the pocket of his letter jacket. "I mean, it's kind of important that I talk to him as soon as possible."

Kat saw fear and nervous excitement in Randy's eyes, and her stomach twisted. "I'll give him a call, okay?"

Kat hurried into her office and punched in Seth's cell number. He picked up almost immediately. "Kat. What's up?"

"I'm not sure." She watched Randy pace the waiting room. "Randy just came in. He says he needs to talk to you. He's…He's really nervous. Almost scared."

"Damn it!" Seth yelled. "Put him on the phone."

"Hold on." She stuck her head out of the office again. "Randy? Seth wants to talk to you."

Randy's hand shook as he took the phone from her. She stepped out of the office, but she could hear Randy's voice, low and urgent. A few moments later, he handed her the phone. "Mr. Anderson wants to talk to you."

"Kat? I'll be there as soon as I can. Keep Randy in your office until then. And don't let anyone else past the front desk."

"Why not?" The urgency in Seth's voice increased her uneasiness. "What's going on?"

But Seth had hung up.

Folding her phone closed, Kat looked at Randy. He was shifting from foot to foot, as if he could barely contain himself. "What's this about, Randy?"

He shook his head. "I can't talk about it. I promised Mr. Anderson I wouldn't." The fear was gone and now only excitement gleamed in his eyes.

"Did Seth tell you to stay here?"

He nodded vigorously. "I'm not supposed to come out for anything. And I won't. I'm supposed to keep the door closed."

"Okay." Dread rolled over her, making her hands shake and her stomach churn as she walked toward the front desk. She heard the snick of the door closing behind her.

Barb was pacing behind the desk, her arms

wrapped around her waist. "What's going on?" she asked when she saw Kat.

"I have no idea." Kat glanced at the closed door of her office again as her anxiety grew. "Neither of them would tell me a thing."

"You talked to Seth?"

"He's on his way over here."

"Is it about Jenna?" Annie asked.

"I don't think so." Kat exchanged a glance with Barb. "I think he would have told us if it was about Jenna."

Ten minutes later the door of the clinic burst open again and a man stormed in. "Where is that little son of a bitch?"

CHAPTER NINETEEN

"CRAIG?" BARB STARED at her boyfriend, bewildered. "What are you talking about?"

"Your brat," he snarled. "Where is he?"

"Randy?"

"How many brats you got?"

Barb recoiled. "What's the matter with you?"

"I need to see him." He stalked to the desk. "Now."

"Craig! You're scaring me." Barb reached toward him, and Kat stepped between them.

"Randy isn't here," she said, folding her arms across her chest. "He's at school."

"Don't give me that crap," Craig growled. "School was over an hour ago."

"What do you want with Randy?" Barb asked. Her shocked look began to fade, replaced by anger. "Just what do you think you're doing, coming to my workplace and making a scene? Get out of here right now." She lifted her chin.

Kat stood next to her receptionist. "Barb's

right," she said evenly. "This is my clinic, and I don't want you here."

"Like I give a damn what you want." He focused his attention on Kat. "You know where he is, don't you, Doc?" He reached across the counter for her, and she batted him away.

"We don't know where Randy is. Get out, Olson." Kat picked up the phone and punched in 911.

Olson grabbed her braid, yanking her closer. "Put the phone down, Doc."

"I don't think so," she said, twisting against his hold. His hand tightened on her hair and the pain made her eyes water.

"Put it down." A black object flashed in the corner of her eye, then something cold and hard pressed against her head.

"Oh, my God!" Barb screamed. "Craig! A gun?"

Kat let the phone drop onto the counter, where it bounced and fell to the floor. Garbled words came out of the handset. Out of the corner of her eye, she saw Annie edge toward the shelves of patient files. *Yes, Annie,* she mentally urged. Her nurse kept her cell phone in her pocket in case her daughter called. If she could get out of sight of Olson, she could call 911.

"Everyone calm down," Craig shouted. "You!" He pointed at Annie. "Get up here. I don't want to hurt anyone. I just want Randy."

"He's not here," Kat managed to say. "Why would we know where he is?"

Craig yanked on her hair. "You shut your mouth, Doc." He nodded at Barb. "She knows where the kid is."

"He's… He's…"

"How would Barb know where Randy is? She's been here all afternoon." Kat drew a shaky breath. She had to stay calm. Stay focused. Seth would be here any minute, and she had to get rid of Olson before he arrived. God knew what Olson would do if Seth walked in the door unexpectedly. "Have you looked at the house?"

"You think I'm stupid?" Olson said with another vicious tug on her hair. "He's not there. But he was. He took something that belongs to me, and I want it back."

"There's nothing of yours at our place," Barb said, glancing at Kat, terror in her eyes.

"Shut up, you stupid cow," he yelled. "You don't know anything."

He smelled of old sweat and sour fear, and Kat gagged as he pulled her nearer. The edge of the counter cut into her side and she stood on her toes to avoid it.

"Mr. Olson. Craig." She grabbed her hair near her scalp, trying to relieve the pressure. "Let me go and calm down. We'll figure this out. Whatever you're missing, I'm sure Randy didn't take it. He's not a thief."

He jammed the gun against her scalp and swore at her, ugly, guttural words filled with anger and desperation. "Tell me where he is, or I start shooting. You'll be first, Doc. Then the brat's mother." He looked at Annie and leered. "I'll save that one for last."

Kat heard a door creak open. "We can't help you, Olson," she said loudly, hoping Randy was sneaking out the back door and trying to cover up the sound. "We can't tell you something we don't know. Maybe, if you calm down, we can figure out where he might have gone."

"You think I'm a fool?" He dragged the top of her body across the counter, and she smelled alcohol on his breath. "Shut up. Only Barb talks."

Kat's hair felt as if it was being ripped out of her scalp. "Stop it," she cried as tears overflowed her eyes. "Let me go."

"As soon as Barb tells me what I want to know."

The front door banged opened. "Hey, Craig." Randy's voice. "You looking for me?"

Olson let go of her hair and Kat slid to the floor. "Get in here, kid."

"No, Randy, run away." Barb sprinted toward her son, but Kat managed to grab her shirt.

"Wait, Barb." Kat twisted her fingers in the cotton fabric. "He's got a gun. Don't move."

"He's going to hurt my baby," Barb cried.

"He won't hurt anyone, Mom." Randy held up what looked like a wad of money. "You want this, Craig? Come and get it."

As Craig lunged for the door and Randy, Kat hauled herself upright and reached for the glass ball Barb used as a paperweight. It had been a gift from Craig. Taking aim, she threw it at him.

It hit Craig in the head and he stumbled on the doorjamb, then fell onto the sidewalk. Randy danced away as Seth leaped from one side of the door, Brady from the other. "Drop the gun," Seth barked.

Olson hesitated, and Seth raised his gun. "Now, Olson."

The man sprawled on the ground finally let the weapon fall from his hands, and Brady kicked it away. Seth held his gun on Olson while Brady patted him down, removing a knife from his pocket. Then Seth cuffed Olson's hands. Brady hauled him upright and Mirandized him.

"Get him out of here," Seth ordered, shoving his weapon into a shoulder holster as he ran into the clinic. "Anyone hurt?" he called out. "Kat?"

"I'm here," she said, pushing away from the wall. "I'm okay. We're all okay, I think."

He shouldered his way past Barb and Randy and pulled her into his arms. His holster nudged her chest, but she wrapped her arms around him and held on, shaking. Seth cupped her face. "You're sure you're okay? He didn't hurt you?"

"He was yanking her around by her hair. Really hard," Annie said in a small voice. "She's probably bruised, too. He banged her into the counter."

"I'm fine, Annie," Kat said. But Annie was right. Her head throbbed as if hot irons were stabbing into her and her ribs felt as if she'd been hit with a brick.

Seth grabbed the phone off the floor. "You still there?" he barked into it. "Send an ambulance." He hung up the phone and lowered her into a chair. "Sit still until they get here."

"I don't need an ambulance," she said.

Seth glanced up at Annie, and she said, "Yes, she does."

"Stay there," he said to Kat. His eyes assessed her and his voice was flat and hard. A cop's voice. She'd never seen this side of Seth. He stood up and looked at Annie, but he didn't let go of Kat's hand. "You okay?"

"I'm fine. He never touched me."

"Barb? Randy?"

"He never touched either of us," Barb said.

"Okay." Seth twined his fingers with Kat's and moved so his body was touching hers. As if he needed reassurance she was there. He glared at Randy. "What the hell were you thinking, Randy? I told you not to touch the money. I said I was getting a search warrant."

"Why were you talking to Randy about this?" Barb asked. "Why didn't you come to me?"

"You were still a suspect," Seth told her bluntly.

Barb paled. "A suspect for what?"

Seth ignored her and said to Randy, "Well?"

"I saw where he kept it, but he started acting weird." Randy shifted from foot to foot. "I was afraid he was going to take off with it. I was bringing it to you."

Seth's hand tightened on Kat's, then he let her go and walked over to Randy. He put his hands on the boy's shoulders. "I told you I didn't want you taking any chances. I didn't want you involved."

Randy shrugged. "I was already involved," he muttered.

Seth sighed. "It worked out this time," he said. "But if you ever pull a stunt like that again, I'll personally kick your ass."

"Now I'm scared, man." Randy grinned.

"It took a lot of guts to open the door and confront Olson. That was a brave thing to do."

Randy shrugged, but his face reddened. "It wasn't a big deal."

"It was a very big deal. You kept your head and did the smart thing by calling me on the cell phone. I'm proud of you, Randy." Seth glanced at Kat and Barb and Annie. "Who threw the paperweight?"

"Dr. Mac," Randy said. "I saw her wind up and let it fly."

"Kat?"

Kat smiled shakily. "Little League. I was a pitcher."

Finally his eyes softened. "Yeah? Nice shot. Looks like you've still got it."

Barb grabbed Seth's arm. "What's going on? Why did you put my son in danger? What's this about?"

"You have a right to know, especially after what just happened. Craig Olson has been passing counterfeit money in Sturgeon Falls and the rest of Door County. A lot of it went through this practice. He used Randy to do it for him."

"Randy?" Barb stared at her son, horrified. "You were passing counterfeit money?"

"Randy didn't know it was counterfeit," Seth said. "Olson told him he was having trouble breaking hundreds. He had Randy bring them here, put them in the cash box and take out a hundred dollars in smaller bills. He gave him twenty bucks every time he did."

"Why did you do that, Randy? You hate Craig," Barb said.

Randy shrugged. "I didn't mind taking his money."

Kat's head throbbed and it was hard to think. But suspicion twisted in her belly. "How did you know about the counterfeit money?" she asked carefully.

"Your bank found it and contacted the Secret Service." Seth's arm tightened around her, but he didn't meet her eyes. "By the time I got here, a number of the phony bills had passed through your practice."

"So you knew about the counterfeit money before you came to Sturgeon Falls." She felt as though she'd been kicked in the chest.

"Yes."

Just one word. But it brought her world crashing down. "I see."

"No, you don't," he said.

She shoved him away. "You've been using us. All of us. That's why you came here, isn't it? Because of the counterfeiting. It had nothing to do with Regan."

"Regan?" Barb asked.

"He's Regan's father. He *said* he came here to make sure I was good enough to take care of her," Kat said, anger and pain roiling together inside her until she could barely breathe.

"*What? Regan's father?*" Barb said.

Seth's face was devoid of expression. "Kat, can we talk about this later? In private?"

"We'll talk about it now, damn it."

The others were visibly uncomfortable. "Why don't we leave you guys alone?" Barb said.

"You need to stick around and talk to the

police," Seth answered. He reached for Kat's hand, but she moved out of his reach. "Let's go outside," he said to Kat.

"We'll go outside." Barb grabbed her son and Annie. "You two stay here and, ah, work this out."

The door shut behind them and Kat turned on Seth. "How could you?" she asked in a low voice. "How could you betray us like that?"

He closed his hands around her shoulders and she jerked away. His touch felt like ice against her skin. "Don't touch me."

"Kat, I can explain. Please."

"Explain what? How you used me? Used Regan?" She choked back a sob. "You used your daughter to investigate me." She thought she knew what pain felt like. She'd had no idea. "You used what we felt for you to solve your case."

"I was going to tell you," he said in a low voice.

"Right." Anger boiled up, rushing through her like a bitter drug. "After you were sure it wasn't me who was passing the counterfeit money."

"It was my job, Kat."

"Is that what it was?" She shoved his chest when he tried to touch her. "Then your job came with first-class perks, didn't it? Hot meals and a warm bed. Nice work if you can get it."

"Making love with you was not a *perk*." Anger

sparked in his eyes. "It was real. It had nothing to do with my job."

"And I'd know that because you've been so honest and upfront with me all along?" Tears prickled her eyes but she refused to let them fall. "What about Regan? Was anything you did or said to her real?"

"Of course it was. Everything was real. She's my daughter. I love her."

"You love her because she has your DNA," she cried. "You don't love *her*."

"You don't think so?" His eyes were hot with anger now, and she welcomed it. Anger was better than his frightening control.

"I don't know how you feel about either of us."

"Then you haven't been paying attention. I admit I didn't love her at first. Why would I? I didn't know her. I wasn't interested in having a child. I didn't want the responsibility. The emotion. I didn't want to feel anything. Then I met you. And Regan. You changed my world. Both of you."

"Then why didn't you tell me what was going on? Why didn't you trust me with the truth?" The knowledge that he hadn't twisted in her heart like a knife.

"Two reasons," he said, his voice even. He'd reined in his temper. "First, I didn't want to put you in danger. If you didn't know anything, you'd act that way if something went wrong. Like it did today."

"And the second reason?"

"I didn't want the ugliness of my job to touch you. Or Regan."

"It had already touched us. We were involved. Was your job more important than we were?"

"Of course not," he said impatiently. "But I keep my job separate from my personal life. It's easier that way."

"Easier for you, you mean." She stared at him, hoping to see his temper again. Needing to know that he wanted her enough to fight for her. "You can't keep your life in compartments, Seth, hoping one never touches the other. Life doesn't work that way. It's messy. Things slop over from one compartment to the other. Everything gets twisted together."

"Not if I can help it." He gave her a level look. "And you weren't completely open, either."

"What did I hold back from you?"

"You didn't tell anyone I was Regan's father. I understand why you didn't tell them at the beginning. But why not later?" He took a step toward her. "You didn't trust me, did you? You weren't sure about me. So you held back."

"I didn't hold back anything from you," she said fiercely. "I gave you everything."

"Not quite. Or you would have told everyone who I was."

"I thought I loved you," she said, her voice

breaking. "But I loved the person you wanted me to see. Not the person you really are."

"They're one and the same. I wasn't thinking of my job when we made love. When we played with Regan. When we talked. It wasn't the Secret Service agent who told you about himself. It was me."

"If you had to do it over, would you tell me about your investigation? Would you be open with me? Are you willing to be completely transparent? To share everything of yourself?"

He hesitated, and her heart shattered. "I don't know," he finally said. "I don't know if I can share everything. I'm just not built that way." He massaged his leg. "I wouldn't know how."

"And you don't even want to try, do you?" she said. "I can't live with a man who isn't willing to give one hundred percent." Even if she was willing to settle for less, she'd resent him eventually. And he'd resent her for wanting more than he was able to give. "If you decide not to sign those papers, if you decide you want to take Regan away from me, I'll fight you. I won't let my daughter be raised by a man who doesn't know how to let people in. She deserves more than that."

He stared at her for a long time, then stepped away. "I'm not perfect, Kat, but I love you. Completely. If you're looking for perfect, I guess I'm out of the running."

He turned to leave, and she grabbed him. "Where are you going? We're not finished."

"We are for now."

"You're walking away?" Pain and anger twisted inside her. "You won't try to work this out?"

"You're angry. I'm not going to try and reason with you while you're angry. We'll talk about this when you calm down."

"How can you say you love me, then walk away?"

"I can't do this, Kat. I can't fight with you." He opened the door and stepped outside, and the door clicked shut behind him.

Paramedics walked in, but she ignored them. Through the window, she watched Seth walk through the parking lot. She willed him to come back, but he disappeared from view.

CHAPTER TWENTY

TWO LONELY, PAINFUL DAYS LATER, when Kat retrieved the mail from her box, she found a bulky envelope without a return address. She turned it over, looking for clues, but there was nothing to tell her what was inside.

As Regan shed her coat and ran into the kitchen, Kat slowly opened the flap. "Can I have some yogurt, Kat?" Regan called.

"Sure, honey."

Kat pulled out a thick sheaf of papers, folded into threes. Her heart raced as she unfolded it. Regan's adoption papers. She looked at the bottom.

Seth had signed away his parental rights. Regan was hers.

She was still staring at the signature when Regan wandered into the room. She stopped when she saw Kat and touched her face. "Why are you crying, Kat? Is something wrong?"

"No, sweetheart. Nothing's wrong."

Regan peered at the papers. "Is that from Seth? Is he coming to see us today?"

Kat smoothed her hand over the top sheet. "No, honey. I don't think he is."

"I miss him."

She drew Regan into her arms. "I miss him, too."

KAT WALKED TO THE FRONT DESK late the next afternoon and found Brady at the counter, leaning over to kiss Annie. He straightened when he saw her.

"Hey, Kat. How are you doing?"

"I'm great." She forced a smile and bit back the questions she wanted to ask about Seth. "And I guess I don't have to ask how you are."

Brady grinned. "Nope. I've never been better."

Kat laid the patient folders down. "Are you two going out tonight?"

"Yes." Annie gave Brady a dreamy look. "This is Hayley's night with Dylan and Charlotte."

"Have fun," Kat said, her chest tight.

As she was getting ready to leave, gathering her purse and jacket in the office, Annie walked in. "What are you still doing here?" Kat asked.

"I wanted to make sure you were okay," Annie answered.

"I'm fine." Kat didn't look at her nurse.

"I don't think you are," Annie said quietly. "It's Seth, isn't it?"

Kat sank onto her chair. "How come you're still with Brady?" she asked. "You told me he dated you because Seth told him to. That Brady was supposed to check you out."

Annie grinned. "And he's done plenty of checking."

"Weren't you angry? Didn't you feel as if he betrayed you?"

Annie's smile faded. "I did, at first. I was hurt that he asked me out as part of an investigation. I didn't like being used. I wondered if anything between us was real." Annie nudged a pen on the desk. "I did my share of crying. But once I calmed down, I realized it didn't matter why he asked me out that first time. I was interested in him before Seth showed up, and he was attracted to me, as well. Seth may have pushed him to ask me out, but he would have done it eventually anyway. And none of that mattered after our first date. By the time everything blew up, I was in love with him. And he was in love with me. No matter how it started, what we felt was real and I didn't want to throw that away."

"Was it that easy to forgive him?"

Annie grinned again. "Maybe not easy. I made him crawl." Her eyes twinkled. "On the plus side, the make-up sex was great."

Kat tried to smile. "I'm glad things are okay between you and Brady."

Annie turned to leave, then hesitated. "Seth's still here, you know. He and Brady are tying up the loose ends of the case. Craig Olson wasn't working alone."

"I didn't know that," she said. "Poor Barb. She seems to be handling it well, though."

"Yeah, *Barb's* doing great." Annie gave her a sharp look. "Two of us are handling it real well."

"Thanks, Annie." Kat pretended to be busy with her calculator until Annie left the office. Then she rested her forehead in her hand and thought about Seth.

LATER THAT EVENING, KAT STOOD at Regan's bedroom door and looked at her daughter sleeping. She was curled up beneath the covers, her dark blond hair tousled around her face. A book lay near her hand, as if she'd been holding it when she'd fallen asleep. Kat leaned into the room and saw it was the butterfly book.

Her heart aching, she watched until she felt her mother's hand on her shoulder. "She'll be fine," Frances murmured.

"I don't know, Mom. She misses her father."

Frances turned her around and held her arms. "You miss him, too. You've been so unhappy, Kat. Are you going to fix that tonight?"

"I hope so. But I still don't understand how he could walk away from us."

"Macauleys yell and fight and thrash things out, then they kiss and make up." Frances's smile was tender and full of memories. "And you're definitely a Macauley. Your father and I have certainly had our share of fights, and it wasn't easy. It's scary to fight when you're afraid the other person might walk away." She kissed Kat's cheek. "Maybe he doesn't understand that you can fight with someone you love and they'll still love you. Remember that, Katriona."

"I told him I loved him. I didn't want him to walk away."

"He knew how much he had to lose, and he's scared." Frances cupped her cheek. "Have you looked at it from his point of view?"

"Maybe he changed his mind," Kat whispered. Maybe she'd scared him with her temper. Why else would he have stayed away?

"You need to ask him," Frances said.

"I know."

Frances pulled Regan's door closed. "Go and see him, Kat. I'll be here for Regan." She grinned mischievously. "Even if I have to stay all night."

THE DUNES MOTEL SAT OFF Highway 42 in an area of scrub bushes and overgrown, abandoned orchards.

The two-story building was pleasant—freshly painted and surrounded by white pines. But the only sand near the building was in the child's sandbox on the dilapidated playground, and Lake Michigan was at least a mile away. Clearly, the government didn't splurge for its employees' accommodations.

Kat rolled to a stop and stared at room 15. The light was on, and Seth's car was parked in front of the door. How would he react? Would he be glad to see her? Would he be angry? Would he tell her it was too late?

Taking a deep breath, she knocked on the door. Time to reach for what she wanted.

"Come on in."

She pushed the door open and saw Seth sitting in one of the hard vinyl chairs by the window. He froze when he saw her.

"Kat. What are you doing here?" He sank back into the chair.

His face was pale and drawn with pain—just like the first night he'd come to her door. "What's wrong? Are you all right?"

"I'm fine." His gaze traveled over her face, as intimate as a touch. "What can I do for you? Is something wrong?"

"Of course something is wrong," she said. She wanted to break down the barriers, but she wasn't sure how to do it. Worse, she was beginning to understand that she was just as responsible for those barriers as he was. "I've missed you, Seth. Regan misses you, too."

"I miss both of you."

"Then why didn't you call me? Or Regan?" This was her fault as much as his. Pain and sorrow twisted together, a tight knot of misery inside her.

"It was clear I couldn't be the man you wanted. I'm not touchy-feely. I never have been." He reached for a glass of amber liquid on the table. "You and Regan deserve more than I can give you."

"That's not true." She stared at him, appalled. "That's not what I meant."

"It's what you said. And you're right. You deserve someone who's as open, as loving as you are."

"I want *you*, Seth." She reached for his hand, curled her fingers around his callused palm. "I love you."

He took another drink, but she thought his lips curved behind the rim of the glass. "Is that why you're yelling at me?"

"I'm yelling because I'm mad at myself. I'm an idiot. I didn't understand." She shifted closer to him. "You don't want to fight, do you? Is it because you're afraid I'll stop loving you if you do?"

He tried to pull his hand away, but she tightened her hold on him.

"Fighting doesn't accomplish anything, Kat."

"It clears the air. It gets the problems out into the open, where we can deal with them. That's how it works, Seth. It doesn't mean we stop loving each other."

"There are better ways of solving problems than fighting," he said.

"You're right. There are." She twined their fingers and kept her gaze on his eyes. He looked a little less alone than when she'd walked into the room. A little less desolate. "But I have a temper. And I'm going to lose it sometimes. Are you going to be able to deal with that?"

"You don't know what you're asking for," he said.

"Yeah, Seth, I do." She brought his hand to her mouth, took a deep breath. Nothing had ever been so important. "Fighting is scary. It's risky. But I promise you, it doesn't matter what you say. I'm not going to walk away, no matter what. I'm in your life, and you're stuck with me."

He drained the glass of liquor and struggled to his feet. Then he reached down, picked up a pair of crutches and hobbled over to the dresser, where he grabbed a bottle of scotch by the neck and then swung back to the chair.

"Seth!" She stared at him, frightened. "Why are you on crutches? What happened to your leg?"

"It's not important." He started to pour the scotch into his glass and she grabbed it away from him.

"What's going on?"

"If we're going to fight, I need another drink."

She set the bottle back on the dresser. "What's wrong with your leg?" she asked quietly.

"It's not a big deal. Just a slightly torn muscle. It happened while we were taking Olson down."

"Are you sure? Who did you see? Can I take a look at it?"

"Don't worry about it, Kat. I'm fine."

Seeing him on crutches, knowing he'd had to deal with the pain and the worry by himself, made her heart ache.

"You shouldn't be drinking if you're taking painkillers."

"I'm not taking any pills," he said.

"I'm so sorry, Seth."

He shrugged. "I told you, it's not a big deal. A couple of weeks on crutches and I'll be good to go."

"I meant I'm sorry you had to deal with it alone."

"That's not a big deal, either."

"Yes, it is," she said. He'd dealt with everything in his life alone. He'd lost his mother; he'd struggled through the foster-care system; he'd made a career for himself as a Secret Service agent and he'd dealt with a devastating injury. All alone.

"No wonder you don't know how to share yourself. No wonder you can't open up to people," she said softly. "You've never done it before."

"Never wanted to."

"It's never been safe for you to open up, has it? I'm so sorry, Seth, that I didn't see that earlier. That I didn't come to you as soon as I did. Can you ever forgive me?"

"Nothing to forgive. You were right. I was using you. And Regan." He took another drink. "It takes a cold SOB to use his own kid in an investigation."

"You're not cold." She moved the glass out of his reach. "And you weren't using Regan. You were using my relationship to her."

"That makes it better?"

He was punishing himself far more than she ever could. "I was wrong, Seth. I didn't understand. I've never had to protect myself. I've always known I was loved. I've always had a stable, happy home. It's easy to share who you are when there are no risks involved. It's a lot harder when being open and loving is used against you."

"You were right. I didn't open up to you."

"Yes, you did," she said. "You told me about yourself. About growing up. About what happened to your mother." Things she knew he'd never told anyone else.

"But I didn't pass the big test, did I?"

"*You* passed with flying colors," she answered. "I'm the one who failed." She took a step closer, touched his face. "You did everything you could to protect Regan and me. You kept us safe. Because you loved us. And because that's what you do. But all I could see was that you hadn't been completely open with me. And that's what I focused on." She stepped closer. "I wasn't thinking of you, Seth. I was thinking of myself. Of how I am. Not about you and the kind of person you are."

"What are you saying, Kat?" The guarded look in his eyes eased just a little.

"I love you, Seth. I hope you can forgive me." She fumbled in her purse. "And by the way, thank you for signing the adoption papers, but I don't want them." She held out the folded bundle. He stared at them for a long moment. But he didn't take them.

"Of course you do. She's all you wanted from me, and now she's yours."

"She's not all I want from you. I want a lot more than Regan."

"What, Kat? What do you want?"

"I want you, Seth. You said I wanted a perfect man, but I don't. Perfect is boring. Perfect would drive me crazy in about two weeks. I want you, flaws and all." She stepped closer and wound her arms around his neck. "I have a few flaws of my own. You probably haven't noticed, but I have a bit of a temper."

For the first time, she saw a glimmer of a smile. "I thought you were the most even-tempered woman in Door County."

"When I'm sleeping, maybe." She cupped his face in her hands. "I hurt you because I didn't *see* you, and I'll be sorry about that for the rest of my life. Can you forgive me?"

"Of course I forgive you." He dropped the crutches on the floor and wrapped his arms around her. "I love you, Kat." He kissed her and desire heated her blood. She pressed closer, close enough to feel the pounding of his heart. Close enough to hear his ragged breathing.

"You shouldn't be standing," she murmured after a while, nuzzling his ear.

"Is that your professional opinion?" He cupped her hips in his hands and slid his mouth along her neck, nipped at the tendon there.

"It is. You need to be lying down. On a bed. With me."

He hobbled over to the bed and drew her down with him. "That's the kind of diagnosis I can get behind."

"Mmm." She kissed his lips, trailed her mouth over his cheek, burrowing her hand beneath his shirt. "I was thinking more about face-to-face."

"Face-to-face works for me," he whispered. "We can save the kinky stuff for later."

She grinned and reached for the buttons of his shirt, but he grabbed her hand and eased away, suddenly serious again. "Are you sure about this, Kat? About me? Because you were right. I don't know how to do this. How to love you. Or Regan. Will you help me?"

"We'll help each other. I've never been more sure of anything in my life." She grabbed the collar of his shirt and brought his face close. "Don't you dare try to leave me again, Seth Anderson. Because if you do, I will hunt you down like a dog and drag you home."

"Promise?"

"Yes. I promise, Seth. Whatever happens, I'll be there. Next to you. Loving you."

"I like the sound of that." He relaxed and nibbled at her mouth. "You do realize there are conditions, don't you?"

"Conditions?"

"It's going to take a long time to teach me everything I need to know about love. A very long time. So I'm going to need a lifetime commitment."

She brushed her mouth over his. "I hope that's nonnegotiable."

"It's airtight."

A long time later, as they lay twined together in

bed, their hearts slowing, he raised himself on his elbows. "I quit the Secret Service."

"What?" She pulled herself up beside him. "Why did you do that?"

He took her hand and pressed her palm to his mouth. "Because you're here. Regan's here, and I couldn't bear to leave either of you. So I resigned."

"We could have worked something out," she said.

"You think I would make you close your practice? Agree to see each other on weekends? Not going to happen."

"What are you going to do?"

"I'll be working for a security firm up here. Gabe was thrilled that I wanted to work for him. So when can we get married?"

"As soon as possible," Kat said. She glanced at the clock, then sat up and scrambled for her clothes. "I don't like leaving you at night."

As he walked her out to her car, he said, "When should we tell Regan?"

"How about tomorrow?" she said. "We can tell her we'll be a family."

"Family." He held her tightly. "My new favorite word."

EPILOGUE

The following April

SETH WAS WAITING FOR HER when she opened the front door. "How did it go?" he murmured as he swept her into his arms.

She wrapped her arms around him and held on tight, absorbing his strength and his comfort. Letting him soothe away the tears.

"It was hard," she finally said. "So hard. But Jenna and Randy were strong, and Barb was a rock for them. Even Jenna's parents were there."

"How are Jenna and Randy doing?" he asked.

"There were a lot of tears, but they know they did the right thing. The best thing for the baby." She smiled up at him. "Zachary. That's what the Claytons named him."

"And they'll be able to see him?"

"Maybe when he's older. But they'll get pictures every month."

"Randy and Jenna were incredibly brave. I hope they know that. I hope they understand the gift they gave the Claytons."

"I saw their faces as they said goodbye to Zachary," Kat said, remembering both the love and the pain. "They know."

They clung together, comforting each other. Suddenly Regan screamed, "Daddy! Daddy! Look what happened."

They broke apart and ran toward Regan's room. "What?" they said together.

Regan held up the long, screen-enclosed butterfly house. "There's a butterfly!"

A single Painted Lady fluttered against the screen, its black-edged orange wings opening and closing slowly.

"One of them hatched." Seth sank onto the floor next to Regan and pulled her close.

"It's beautiful," Regan breathed.

Seth glanced up at Kat, then smoothed Regan's hair. "It sure is."

"Can we keep it?" Regan asked.

"It would die if we kept it," Seth answered. "You don't want that, do you?"

"No." She touched a finger to the cage where the butterfly clung, and it flew to another spot. "We'll let it go."

"How about right now?" Kat said.

"Okay."

Kat took the butterfly house as Regan scrambled to her feet. Seth stood, moving smoothly. His leg had healed almost completely. The three of them walked into the backyard.

"Ready?" Regan asked.

They nodded and she opened the top of the container. The Painted Lady didn't move, so Regan touched the screen again, and it fluttered out into the spring air. It landed on a purple pansy and rested there for a moment. Then, silhouetted against a heartbreakingly blue sky, it drifted away.

"Goodbye, Painted Lady," Regan called. She watched until it disappeared.

Seth picked up Regan with one arm and slipped the other around Kat's waist, resting it on the tiny bulge that had just begun to show. "She's gone off to find another butterfly and live happily ever after," he said to Regan.

"Just like us?" Regan rested her head on his shoulder as she watched the butterfly dance among the flowers.

"Yes, sweetheart," he said. "Just like us."

Kimberley Blackstone didn't notice the waiting horde of media until it was too late. Flashbulbs exploded around her like a New Year's light show. She skidded to a halt, so abruptly her trailing suitcase all but overtook her.

This had to be a case of mistaken identity. Surely. Kimberley hadn't been on the paparazzi hit list for close to a decade, not since she'd estranged herself from her billionaire father and his headline-hungry diamond business.

But no, it was *her* name they called. *Her* face was the focus of a swarm of lenses that circled her like avid hornets. Her heart started to pound with fear-fueled adrenaline.

What did they want?

What was going on?

With a rising sense of bewilderment she scanned the crowd for a clue, and her gaze fastened on a tall, leonine figure forcing his way to the front. A tall, familiar figure. Her head came up in stunned recognition, and their gazes collided across the sea of heads before the cameras erupted with another barrage of flashes, this time right in her exposed face.

Blinded by the flashbulbs—and by the shock of that momentary eye-meet—Kimberley didn't realize his intent until he'd forged his way to her side, possibly by the sheer strength of his personality. She felt his arm wrap around her shoulder, pulling her into the protective shelter of his body, allowing her no time to object. No chance to lift her hands to ward him off.

In the space of a hastily drawn breath, she found herself plastered knee-to-nose against six-feet-two-inches of hard-bodied male.

Ric Perrini.

Her lover for ten torrid weeks, her husband for ten tumultuous days.

Her ex for ten tranquil years.

After all this time, he should not have felt so familiar but, oh, dear, he did. She knew the scent of that body and its lean, muscular strength. She knew its heat and its slick power and every response it could draw from hers.

She also recognized the ease with which he'd taken control of the moment and the decisiveness of his deep voice when it rumbled close to her ear. "I have a car waiting outside. Is this your only luggage?"

Kimberley nodded. "I assume you will tell me," she said tightly, "what this welcome party is all about."

"Not while the welcome party is within earshot. No."

Barking a request for the cameramen to stand aside, Perrini took her hand and pulled her into step with his ground-eating stride. Kimberley let him, because he was right, damn his arrogant, Italian-suited hide. Despite the speed with which he whisked her across the airport terminal, she could almost feel the hot breath of the pursuing media on her back.

This was neither the time nor the place for explanations. Inside his car, however, she would get answers.

Now that the initial shock had been blown away—by the haste of their retreat, by the heat of her gathering indignation, by the rush of adrenaline fired by Perrini's presence and the looming verbal battle—her brain was starting to tick over. This had to be her father's doing. And if it was a Howard Blackstone publicity ploy, then it had to be about Blackstone Diamonds, the company that ruled his life.

The knowledge made her chest tighten with a familiar ache of disillusionment.

She'd known her father would be flying in from Sydney for today's opening of the newest in his chain of exclusive, high-end jewelry boutiques. The opulent shopfront sat adjacent to the rival business where

Kimberley worked. No coincidence, she thought bitterly, just as it was no coincidence that Ric Perrini was here in Auckland ushering her to his car.

Perrini was Howard Blackstone's right-hand man, second in command at Blackstone Diamonds, a legacy of his short-lived marriage to the boss's daughter. No doubt her father had sent him to fetch her; the question was *why?*

* * * * *

Get swept away down under with the glitz and glamour of the Blackstone empire as Kimberley tries to determine the real reason behind her "reunion" with Ric....

*Look for VOWS & A VENGEFUL GROOM
by Bronwyn Jameson,
in stores January 2008.*

Silhouette®

Desire

When Kimberley Blackstone's father is presumed dead, Kimberley is required to take over the helm of Blackstone Diamonds. She has to work closely with her ex, Ric Perrini, to battle not only the press, but also the fierce attraction still sizzling between them. Does Ric feel the same...or is it the power her share of Blackstone Diamonds will provide him as he battles for boardroom supremacy.

Look for

VOWS & A VENGEFUL GROOM

by

BRONWYN JAMESON

Available January wherever you buy books

Executive Sue Ellen Carson was ordered by her boss
to undergo three weeks of wilderness training run
by retired USAF officer Joe Goodwin. She was there
to evaluate the program for federal funding approval.
But trading in power suits for combat fatigues was
hard enough—fighting off her feelings for Joe was
almost impossible....

Look for

RISKY BUSINESS

by

MERLINE
LOVELACE

Available January wherever you buy books

HARLEQUIN®

N𝑒xt™

TheNextNovel.com

HN88149

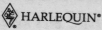

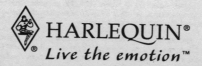

REQUEST YOUR FREE BOOKS!
2 FREE NOVELS PLUS 2 FREE GIFTS!

HARLEQUIN®

Super Romance®

Exciting, emotional, unexpected!

YES! Please send me 2 FREE Harlequin Superromance® novels and my 2 FREE gifts. After receiving them, if I don't wish to receive any more books, I can return the shipping statement marked "cancel." If I don't cancel, I will receive 6 brand-new novels every month and be billed just $4.69 per book in the U.S., or $5.24 per book in Canada, plus 25¢ shipping and handling per book and applicable taxes, if any*. That's a savings of close to 15% off the cover price! I understand that accepting the 2 free books and gifts places me under no obligation to buy anything. I can always return a shipment and cancel at any time. Even if I never buy another book from Harlequin, the two free books and gifts are mine to keep forever.   135 HDN EEX7 336 HDN EEYK

Name	(PLEASE PRINT)	
Address		Apt.
City	State/Prov.	Zip/Postal Code

Signature (if under 18, a parent or guardian must sign)

Mail to the Harlequin Reader Service®:
IN U.S.A.: P.O. Box 1867, Buffalo, NY 14240-1867
IN CANADA: P.O. Box 609, Fort Erie, Ontario L2A 5X3

Not valid to current Harlequin Superromance subscribers.

Want to try two free books from another line?
Call 1-800-873-8635 or visit www.morefreebooks.com.

* Terms and prices subject to change without notice. NY residents add applicable sales tax. Canadian residents will be charged applicable provincial taxes and GST. This offer is limited to one order per household. All orders subject to approval. Credit or debit balances in a customer's account(s) may be offset by any other outstanding balance owed by or to the customer. Please allow 4 to 6 weeks for delivery.

Your Privacy: Harlequin is committed to protecting your privacy. Our Privacy Policy is available online at www.eHarlequin.com or upon request from the Reader Service. From time to time we make our lists of customers available to reputable firms who may have a product or service of interest to you. If you would prefer we not share your name and address, please check here. ☐

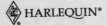

HARLEQUIN
Super Romance

COMING NEXT MONTH